# THE ORLELL CHRONICLES

## Book 1

# Guardians

## of

# Gayrile

Alice G. Bjornstedt

*For my brothers, for encouraging me to finish the story,*

*for my mom, for the suggestions and edits that made it better,*

*and for my dad, for reading the final product.*

# *Also in the Orlell Chronicles*

Book 1 - Guardians of Gayrile

Book 2 - The Jewel of Power

Book 3 - The Quest for Drisilas

Book 4 - The Shard and the Shadow

Book 5 - The Curse of the Compass

Book 6 - The Prophecy of Three

Book 7 - The Song of the Stars

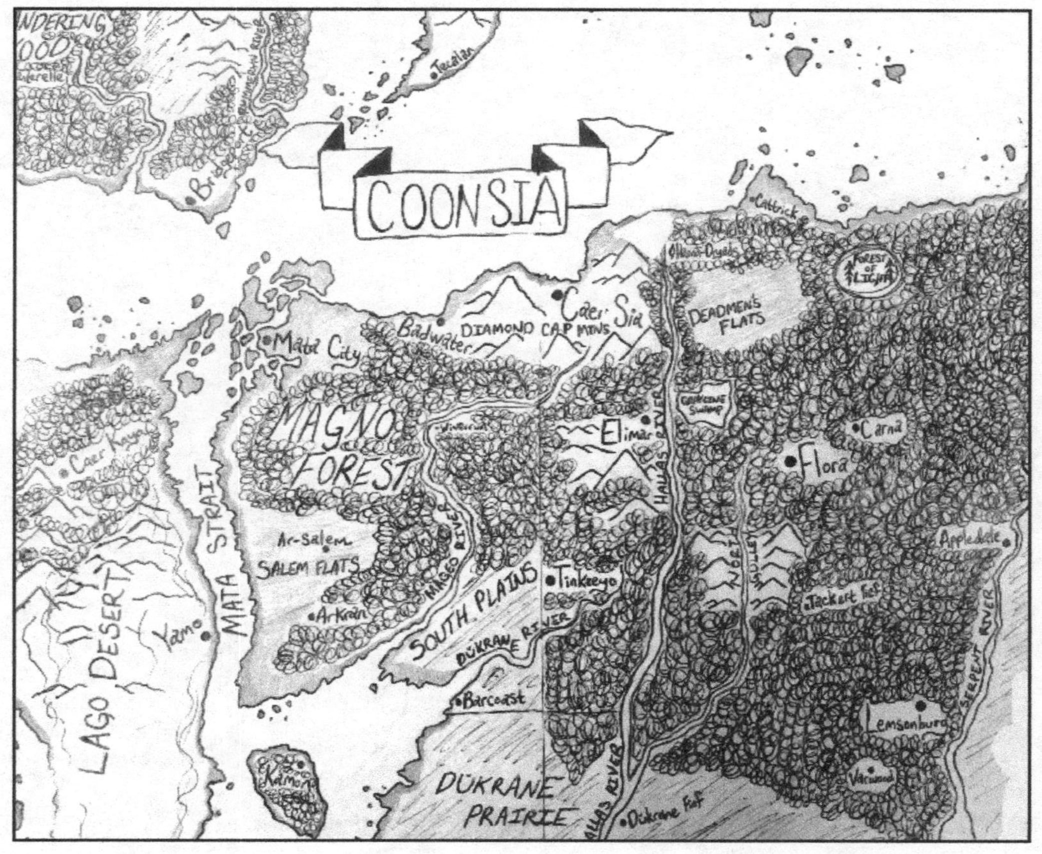

LAGO DESERT
MATA STRAIT
COONSIA
SALEM FLATS
Ar-Salem
Ar-Kaln
MAGNO FOREST
Mata City
SOUTH PLAINS
DUKRANE PRAIRIE
Burcaast
MAGEO RIVER
DUKRANE RIVER
ALLAS RIVER
Tinkeep
HALLAS RIVER
Eimar
Badwater
DIAMOND CAP MINES
Caer Sia
DEADMEN'S FLATS
NORTH VALLEY
SERPENT RIVER
Flora
Carna

# Table of Contents

# Prologue


*In the castle of Caer Sia, capital of Coonsia, early evening...*

Winter was coming, riding on the shoulders of a dreary mist of rain right before nightfall. Only the two guards, standing and shivering on the castle walls, saw the rider emerge from the darkness.

Castle Sia had little reason to expect visitors at this time of day—less so in these times. Life had been uneventful since the fall of the tyrannical queen some thirteen years prior. Blissfully quiet. Boring even. Silent. But it was the kind of silence that left everyone on edge.

The rider bent over the horse's neck, urging her forward with a few gentle words, his voice rasping and dry. "Just a little farther, girl," Dandio Ki, brother of the High King, and leader of Caer Sia's military, whispered softly. The horse snorted at the sound of her master's voice and continued forward.

No, the silence wasn't a peaceful one, he thought to himself as the horse raised her head and trotted the remaining distance to the castle walls. Not in the least. He had sensed that by now, after hearing little from the Northern Isles in these recent months.

The larger island of the two Northern Isles, Gayrile, was a Coonsian territory, and had seen its share of difficulties during the last twelve years. The country had been aided, or so they assumed, by a select few who had founded a sect of defending warriors.

Keepers of the peace, protectors of the common folk. Guardians.

And so they kept the peace for nearly a decade… now something had interrupted that.

The drawbridge lowered as the rider approached, and the guards milling about in the courtyard stiffened uneasily as the horse clattered inside. The rider dismounted, swinging down from the saddle, his long sword tapping his leg as he walked briskly toward the castle doors. His hood fell back as he did, and the guards relaxed as they recognized him.

"Sir…" one of them started.

Dandio turned to him, the torchlight highlighting his face as he smiled wearily. Silver-toned skin, green eyes, and a long scar that ran down the length of the right side of his face. "Good to see you, Private. Do you mind letting me in?"

The private nodded to the gatekeepers, who swung open the heavy doors, then looked back at the newcomer. "The king's been expecting you. You… you went to Badwater, right? How's the situation there?"

The silence that fell told him that everyone in the courtyard was listening. Badwater, a small town along the northern coast about thirty miles from Caer Sia, was the closest source of news about the Northern Isles.

Dandio took a long breath. "Nothing good," he said finally, and slipped inside the castle.

The palace bustled with activity of early evening. He brushed past servants carrying trays of unwashed dishes and baskets of linen, past courtiers gossiping in the halls, and paused to nod a greeting to one of his generals. But he hadn't come to speak with any of them.

He reached the end of the hall and turned left, into the throne room. The room was strikingly quiet after the bustle of the halls, and completely deserted. For a moment he hesitated, not sure where else to look for his brother.

Then the king's voice, calm and clear, and sounding rather weary, came from behind him.

"Ah, good, Dandio. Forgive me, I was speaking with the guards."

Dandio turned, clasping one gauntleted hand to his chest in salute before embracing his brother. "Not to worry. Good to see you."

"You as well." Ĵan Ki, the High King of the Liznees of Coonsia, looked at his younger brother carefully. Despite the lavish riches of Caer Sia, Ĵan wore a simple suit of dark leather, with red and silver inlays that echoed the nation's flag colors. His keen green eyes, nearly identical to his brother's, were filled with concern. Both Liznees had silver skin and no hair on their heads or face, like all Liznee males.

"Badwater is doing well enough," Dandio told him now, as they moved toward the center of the room. "Despite their trade routes being interrupted, that is."

Ĵan looked at him sharply. "Their trade routes? Then…"

"It's true," Dandio said heavily. "All of it, everything about Gayrile turning on us… this Safacon person is no mere politician, and he's taken total control of that little island."

"What of the Direns? Surely they will fight."

"The Diren kingdom cannot be troubled with war again, you know this—not after the last queen. They are still recovering."

Jan bit his lip. Gayrile was a Coonsian territory—therefore, it was their duty to protect it. Something would have to be done.

"What of the Guardians?"

Dandio took a breath. "This Safacon… he has great power. He disbanded the Guardians almost the moment he was elected. Forced them into hiding, I've heard."

Jan shook his head grimly. "Then it is up to us. We will help Gayrile."

Dandio paused before speaking again, uncertain about delivering the rest of his news. The news itself was so wild, so unlikely that he wondered if Jan would believe it. But he trusted his brother, and he knew the news needed to be told. "There's something else, Jan… something about one called Kado."

Jan looked at him, frowning slightly. "Kado… he's the one we heard of last week. Safacon's deputy, is he not?"

"Yes, he is. He is also a wizard as well, or so I've heard. Rumor is he was attempting to create an army—an army of undead, immortal warriors."

"Well, that's new," Jan said wryly, shaking his head. It seemed to be the goal of nearly every sorcerer that rose to power lately.

"What of him, then?"

"He's coming. Here. He is bent on taking over Coonsia—Safacon is as well, but he cannot allow his hold on Gayrile to slip, and so he stays there. Kado plans to attack us—his force is coming."

Jan straightened, the implication of this weighing on him. "Very well. In that case we will be ready for him. Any other news?"

The look on Dandio's face told him it wasn't good news even before he spoke.

"The rest of the news is that Kado's experiment worked. His army, the one he wanted to create, the deathless warriors... they exist. And they're on their way."

# 1

∾ ∾ ∾ ∾ ∾ ∾ ∾ ∾ ∾

## *A Story and a Storm*

*Two days later, on Gayrile…*

It was going to rain again.

Rygal, who had grown up in this climate, could practically sense it. He raised his head and allowed the wind to blow salty droplets into his face. The salty scent of the sea, the distant clamor of the market a few miles away from the beach, and the feel of the cold ocean wind as it blew across the North Sea to Gayrile were pieces that made up his home and the life that he had here.

He wove his way through the muddy streets of the township, moving past crowds of people. This area was known simply as the Alley, which aptly described it. It was a narrow road between houses and shops, with the sea directly behind it and the buildings ahead and around. This allowed for a cramped passageway that grew all the more soggy at high tide, when the waves were caught in the wind and blown in soaking droplets into the Alley. It was low tide now, but the coming rain made everything feel damp.

He pushed his way through the crowd, a small, skinny boy with dark hair and blue eyes. It wasn't hard to get past people—he could hear the snatches of conversation as he went, bits of information.

"Can't buy a decent bit of fish anywhere, soldiers say it's for rations…"

"Rations my foot—they take it straight to their boss more like, bet he's sitting up in his lovely palace all fat by now…"

"I assumed he was rotten the whole time and you still supported him, don't complain to me…"

"He's good to us, we're all still alive, aren't we?"

"Safacon could kill us all if he wants to. Don't fool yourself, he's a coldblooded man if ever I saw one…"

"He's a politician, dimwit, they're all like that…"

Rygal slipped on the mud and had to catch the arm of the last speaker to avoid falling, which made the man pull away. "Sorry," he stammered to the man, who eyed him distastefully. Thankfully one of the vendors recognized him.

"Ah, Rygal! Glad to see you, boy."

Rygal stopped, leaning against the side of the shop, grinning. "Oh, hello, Mr. Kellis. Can I buy a loaf?"

The baker, Mr. Kellis, reached below the counter and produced a loaf of day-old bread wrapped in paper. "Here you are, boy. Take it and be going—I have work to get back to. Give my regards to Norrin."

Rygal took the loaf, laid a few coins on the counter and started back down the Alley, toward the sea. The wind blew salt water into his hair and face. Despite the cold, he closed his eyes, relishing the coolness and the closeness of the water.

By the time he reached the little house on the hill overlooking the sea, he was damp through. He pushed through the door, peeking inside.

"Norrin? I got the bread."

He could see the form of the old man by the window, who now turned.

"Ah, thank you, Rygal. How is Mr. Kellis?"

"He was good—he said hello," Rygal reported, placing the now slightly damp bread by the fire. The sofa was positioned next to the fire, with a small table behind it covered in strange tools and objects. Norrin's work, Rygal knew.

"Good to hear." Norrin moved closer to the fire, the light reflecting on his weathered face. He had a small, scruffy beard, short-trimmed hair, and wore the simple garb of a fisherman. His eyes had a quiet light of humor deep in them, a light that had always felt so welcoming and trustworthy. Rygal didn't care that Norrin wasn't his father, didn't care that the old man kept his secrets close. Norrin had raised him since before he could talk, and that was all that really mattered.

Still, he couldn't stop his thoughts from wandering about the past as he set another piece of wood on the fire.

"Did you finish that net of yours?" Norrin asked him, moving back to the table.

Rygal winced. "I… forgot to… didn't have time…" he offered weakly, knowing it was a bad excuse. In truth, he had had plenty of time. The problem was that his time was usually eaten up by other things, things other than fishing.

Norrin turned to him, arching an eyebrow. "Is that so? And what has taken up that time, then?"

Rygal hesitated for far too long—he saw Norrin watching him, and knew it would be impossible to talk around this. "I… I was at the docks yesterday—watched a few ships come in with the Morris boys. We were playing Forts-and-Arrows. Then I went… to Mr. Kellis' shop."

"Oh?" Norrin hid a smile as he adjusted the screws on one of the tools on the table.

"I was listening," Rygal said. "Just listening—I helped him knead some of the dough for the rolls. A few of the fisherman from the Mainland came into port yesterday, and they came by to talk to him." He paused, then looked up at Norrin. "They had news."

Norrin looked at him, then set down the instrument. "Well, tell me about it."

"News from the Mainland. News about how Safacon has broken all ties with the Diren people—I didn't really understand that bit, but is it true that he's… trying to take over?" He saw a flash of uncertainty cross Norrin's face, quickly masked. There was a brief silence.

"You are a very attentive boy," Norrin told him finally. "You listen and you know what is true and what isn't. And you ask your elders for confirmation before making an assumption."

"Well, that's what you've taught me," Rygal said hesitantly. "You said I should always gather facts before making a decision. Not rush in headlong."

"So I tried," Norrin said with a slight smile. Then he became serious. "Well, Rygal, the answer to your question is a long one, I'm afraid. A long story."

Rygal's heart leapt. Norrin's stories were not something to miss. "Can you tell me?"

"Perhaps parts of it." Norrin held the instrument up to the sky, peering through the lens, adjusting it as he did. He muttered something to himself, then set it down again.

"What is that?" Rygal asked curiously.

Norrin glanced up at him and smiled. "An object to measure distance at sea. It is called a sextant. Before Safacon, they were a standard among seafarers. Now, well, only a few have them. The rest were confiscated."

Rygal studied it for a moment, then looked back at Norrin. "Safacon took them? Why?"

"He needed such tools for his army. To better protect the common folk. Or so he said."

"You didn't believe him."

"Few did. There was little choice."

Rygal hesitated before asking his next question. "Did my father?"

Norrin looked up at him. "Your father doubted Safacon's promises, as did many. Unlike the others, well, he chose to do something about it."

"He did?" Rygal stood, suddenly excited. "Did he fight them?"

Norrin set the sextant down and moved near the fire to stand before Rygal.

"It's a long story, as I said, Rygal, but to answer your first question, Safacon is not currently taking over Gayrile. I'm afraid he already has. He wants little doing with the Diren people or their king, despite the alliance. He cares less for Coonsia."

"Why?"

Norrin smiled slightly. "He wants power, Rygal. Most people in such a position do. Unfortunately, however, Safacon poses more threat than an ambitious lord."

There was a moment of silence. Norrin did not elaborate on what sort of threat Safacon would pose to them, so Rygal was left to wonder. The fire crackled. Outside, it had begun to rain harder. The Alley would be swamped by evening, Rygal thought.

"Tell me the story," he said finally. "Please—I want to know."

Norrin sat in his chair, staring into the fire. Rygal sat on the sofa across from him, waiting expectantly.

"It was long ago," Norrin said finally. "Long, long ago, Rygal, in other times. Before I wore the simple guise of a fisherman." He looked up. "Before Safacon, there were warriors. Guardians of Gayrile. We guarded Gayrile's people and towns, keeping the peace and caring for those less fortunate."

Rygal stared at him in awe. He had guessed something along

those lines—Norrin knew too much lore and history, knowledge that was now forbidden to study, to have always been a lowly fisherman. "You were one of them? One of the Guardians?" He had only heard rumors of the legendary warriors of Gayrile.

"So I was," Norrin said with a faint smile.

"Did you—did you do the things the legends say you did? Fight dragons, save princesses, and wield staffs of magic?" Rygal asked eagerly.

Norrin chuckled. "No, many of those tales are false. Most of what we did was simple, and, to your young mind, exceedingly boring. We established treaties, defended the common folk, and every now and then battled a warlord." His face fell. "When Safacon rose to power, he first disbanded and then threatened the lives of the Guardians. We were a threat to him and his rule due to our closeness with the High King."

Rygal looked up, startled. "High King Ĵan, of Coonsia? But I thought Safacon has to listen to him, since Gayrile's a Coonsian territory."

"So he does. But Safacon wields great power, and believes himself capable to eventually take control of first Gayrile, then Coonsia."

Rygal was stunned. "He can't do that. There's no way, right? I mean, the Liznees and their army in Caer Sia will easily defeat him."

"I believe so," Norrin said. "But Safacon has great power in alchemy and other such ancient trades. It has been said that he has created an army of deathless wraiths, which his deputy Kado will lead against Caer Sia."

Rygal frowned, glancing back at the flickering fire. "The Liznees will fight him—they can stop him."

"Are you so sure?" Norrin asked softly.

There was a pause. Rygal turned back to the old man. "What happened to the Guardians?"

"We resisted Safacon when he first rose to power," Norrin said. "He… was far stronger than us. Many of us were killed in that battle, and the Guardians were outlawed and scattered. Safacon put great bounties on the capture of the survivors. He had powerful weapons—cruel devices he had conceived that made our current existence impossible. And so we were forced to go into hiding in the guise of ordinary townsfolk."

Another pause. It was raining harder outside. Rygal's mind lingered on the story, and he thought of the Guardians, of Norrin fighting with them, and of Safacon who brought about their defeat.

"Norrin," he started softly, "who was my father, really?"

He had pondered this question so many times that it felt almost strange to ask it out loud. Norrin had only told him bits and pieces about his father—those pieces fit into a puzzle that didn't yet have a shape.

Norrin was silent for a moment. "He was a good man, and a

great friend," he said at last. "He was with me during a secretive attack that we and another comrade led against Safacon. We… succeeded in that attack. Maran was killed as we retreated."

"Maran," Rygal repeated softly. It had to be the first time he had heard the name spoken aloud.

The wind had picked up outside. Rygal could hear hail pelting against the side of the house. Norrin turned to him, smiling slightly.

"You remind me very much of your father, you know," he said simply. "Your actions, your bravery, the way you look out for the weak—remember that, Rygal. You have a Guardian's blood in your veins, so act wisely."

# 2

## Soldiers in the Marketplace

The rain let up by morning, thankfully. Rygal woke early and walked to the pier. Out here, alone before the open sea, he felt truly alive. The sun was rising to his right, to the east, painting the sky a fiery red.

His thoughts strayed back to last night's conversation. He had a sense that he wouldn't be able to get much more information out of Norrin for a little while—he'd seen the pain in the old man's face when they'd discussed the fall of the Guardians, and he didn't want to press further. Still, he couldn't help feeling curious.

The idea of a time before the lingering threat of Safacon was a fascinating one. And if the Guardians of Gayrile could be rallied again…

He wondered what would happen if such a thing occurred. Maybe Norrin would lead them. Maybe Safacon could be overthrown.

A northern breeze whipped over the pier, blowing his hair back and making his eyes water. That was a rogue breeze, he recalled Norrin saying. A sign of the autumn months coming to a close. Winter was coming.

He didn't remember much about his father, even less about his mother, who had died in childbirth. Norrin had known both his parents, and so most of Rygal's knowledge of them had come from those stories. His mother had been strong, kind, and beautiful—his father Maran had been brave and loyal.

Rygal had a few vague images of his father in his mind—clouded memories of a bearded man, with the same twinkling blue eyes that Rygal had. He could remember a voice too, a deep voice with a hidden note of humor there.

And Safacon had killed him. He wasn't sure how, but it had been done.

He jogged towards the market, where the muted sounds of the township awakening were slowly getting louder. It was the beginning of the week, so market would be busy. Most business in the Alley relied on the market days to draw in the larger crowds. Vendors would gather from the outlying villages to sell their goods.

He reached the market, which was already quite noisy with activity. People talked, shouted, laughed to each other as they moved amongst the vendors.

Norrin would be here soon, he guessed, and would set up his tent to sell his catch of the day.

Rygal sat down to wait, watching the crowds mill around. A sudden commotion to his right made him turn quickly.

Three soldiers, wearing the colors of Safacon, were harassing one of the vendors, a small, slightly built woman. He watched them as they mocked her goods, then her looks; one of them reached forward, gripping her shoulder, his voice low and wicked.

"That's enough!"

Mr. Kellis pushed through the soldiers, taking the woman's hand and pulling her out of the soldier's grasp. Rygal stood, watching, suddenly unsure of why his heart was pounding with nervousness.

The first soldier, the one who had grabbed the woman, stepped forward, towering over Mr. Kellis threateningly. "This don't concern you, baker," he growled. "Now get back to your shop."

Mr. Kellis glared back at him, not letting go of the woman's hand; she stood nervously behind him. "Come with me, dear," he finally said to her, turning away.

The soldier grabbed the back of his coat and wrenched him back with startling intensity. "I said leave off. Let her go or I'll arrest you for harassing this fine young lady."

The woman stammered something—the soldier grinned at her, shaking his head. "Don't worry missy—we'll help you. On our word." He winked and smirked.

Mr. Kellis didn't move—the soldier raised his fist without warning and punched him so hard he staggered back.

"Hey!" Rygal had moved forward without realizing, and stood before the soldiers, quivering with rage. The soldier looked at him in surprise. Rygal's whole body felt hot with anger—he jumped forward, kicking the soldier in the knee, which allowed his hold on the woman to loosen. She quickly pulled herself free and ran.

"You little wretch," the soldier snarled, straightening. His two companions moved forward behind him.

The hot anger was slowly replaced by fear—cold, bitter fear. Rygal turned to run—the soldier seized him by the back of the neck like he weighed no more than a kitten and heaved him to the ground. The second man kicked him in the ribs—Rygal gasped, feeling the air punched out of his lungs, and rolled painfully to his side. Another kick caught him in the shoulder, rolling him back over so that his face was pressed into the mud.

He thought he heard Mr. Kellis shouting something faintly, thought he could hear the soldiers laughing… and then suddenly the anger was back, flaring through him like fire. He rolled out of the way of another kick and got to his feet painfully, raising his fists. The soldiers looked at him and laughed.

The leader stepped forward, watching him carefully, then smiled. "You're a brave little brat, I'll give you that," he said finally. "Who knows, with training you could even join Safacon's great army." He grinned. "What say you to that? Join the army, serve your country, never go a day without food again?"

Rygal glared at him. The food offer was invalid—Norrin had always provided for him. Not much, but he had never gone hungry in his life, which was luckier than a lot of people in this area.

"I'm not in the mood for joining tyrants," he spat without thinking.

The soldier's smile vanished, and he lunged forward. Rygal

dodged out of the way, but one of the other soldiers gripped his neck and flung him down again—he curled into a ball helplessly as the kicking started again.

"Stop!"

This time, a strong voice shouted the order, a familiar voice, a beloved voice. Rygal peeked through his fingers and saw Norrin approaching, carrying several large fish over one shoulder. His other hand gripped the filleting knife, and he had raised it slightly.

The lead soldier grabbed the back of Rygal's tunic and heaved him up to his feet. "This your boy, fisherman? You're lucky he's still alive." His eyes narrowed. "From what he's said, I could arrest you both for treason."

Norrin watched them, his voice calm, but a flash of uncertainty crossed his face. "Treason? How so?"

Rygal felt a sudden surge of fear. Norrin was supposed to be in hiding—if the soldiers found out who he was…

"He's called our noble leader Safacon a tyrant," one of the other soldiers snarled. "That's cause enough for both of you to die, since it's likely you filling his head with such ideas."

"Indeed," Norrin murmured. Rygal had the sense he was doing some very quick thinking. "Well, he is only a boy, sir. In his defense, I myself did not vote for Safacon to be elected to the place he is now, but have since submitted willingly to his authority. I suppose the boy overheard me express some disappointment and hence formed a hasty opinion." He smiled.

"Did you or did you not call him a tyrant?" the warrior demanded.

"I did not. And as I said, despite my not voting for Safacon at the start, I have gotten over my disappointment and have submitted to his rule."

Several tense seconds passed. Two of the soldiers seemed satisfied; their leader was still eying Norrin carefully.

"Well, then," he said at last. "Here's your brat back." He shoved Rygal away. "But know I'll report this to Safacon. If he thinks this is suspicious, I'll be back to kill both of you."

Norrin smiled shortly and nodded. "Warning is duly noted, sir. Thank you." He turned away, striding through the market, handing his fish to Mr. Kellis. "Sell these for me, will you—keep half of the profit yourself, as apology for this mess."

"No harm done, no harm done," the baker told him, glancing back at the soldiers. "You sure you're both…"

"We'll be fine. Have a fine afternoon."

Norrin took Rygal's arm and they started towards the harbor.

"Norrin…" Rygal finally stammered. "Norrin, I'm sorry—I didn't—"

Norrin stopped, taking his shoulders, and looked him up and down. "Are you hurt?"

A trail of blood was running from Rygal's lip, but he wiped it away and shook his head. "No—I'm all right." His whole body felt shaky. Now that the adrenaline and anger had gone, he only felt fearful, remembering the hate in the soldiers' eyes and the strength of their blows. "I—I didn't think—I'm sorry—"

"Calm down," Norrin said gently, producing a soft cloth and cleaning the blood and mud from Rygal's face. He checked Rygal's ribs, which were aching from the kick, but thankfully deemed them bruised, not broken.

"They might come after us," Rygal stammered wretchedly.

Norrin shook his head and put an arm around Rygal as they walked. "They won't find us. I guess that by the end of the day, the soldiers will have something else on their minds, and even if they do report it, they don't know who we are, and Safacon has neither the time nor the want to investigate every single disagreement. Understood?"

"Yes," Rygal said, still feeling miserable. "But…"

"Rygal, what's done is done. There's no amount of worrying that can change that." Norrin looked at him. "But perhaps you could explain to me why it started in the first place. You're normally not one to go charging into fights."

His tone was gentle, and he said it with a smile that made Rygal relax. "They… they were bullying a woman—grabbing her and taunting her. Mr. Kellis told them to stop, and they hit him. And then I jumped in."

"Well, then. You did the right thing, just in the wrong way, I suppose. Nevertheless I'm proud of you, Rygal. I'm glad you spoke up." They reached the harbor. Norrin nodded toward the little skiff. "Let's go. I'll have you work on your netting a bit before it rains again."

Rygal climbed on board the skiff and helped ready the sail, then Norrin guided the boat out of the harbor. Rygal remained silent as the little craft bucked over the waves, moving steadily out to sea. Dark clouds lurked on the horizon, but for now the sea was peaceful.

Norrin showed him how to fling the net out over the water, and how to haul it back in quickly so that the fish wouldn't get out. This took up most of the morning, and the satisfaction of bringing in a catch drove away Rygal's lingering fear and anger from the fight.

They had fished for a little over an hour when it began to rain again. The wind had picked up, rocking the boat from side to side and making further netting impossible.

"Bring them in," Norrin told him, as Rygal cast once more. "It's difficult and dangerous to bring a net back in weather like this. Bring it in."

Rygal had spotted a small school of fish swarm just under where he had flung the net, and had barely heard him. "All right—just a second, I think I caught them…"

He felt a slight change in the boat's motion, and looked up at Norrin, startled. There was a faint rushing sound audible in the water. "What is that, Norrin?"

Norrin had pulled down the sail—with this wind, it would be impossible for them to adjust the sail correctly in time without having it ripped to shreds.

"The Eastern Current," he told him. "It's a current in the sea that occurs year-round—this time of year, it gets closer to the Isles."

The boat heaved as it rounded the pathway of water. Rygal, still holding onto his net, glanced down and could see a stream of bubbles down below, all moving rapidly southeast. Norrin's arms, strengthened from years of boating, wrenched the skiff from the current's grip with a few paddles on the oars, and they were free again. A wave broke over the prow as thunder rumbled overhead.

"Get back from the rail," Norrin cautioned. "Let go of the net— you won't be able to bring it in—"

His voice was muffled by the wind, and Rygal didn't let go—he could see the fish squirming in his net, and was not about to let them go. "Hang on—I've almost got it," he shouted over the rushing water. "One second…"

And that was when everything went wrong.

He never saw the rogue wave as it rose up from behind him, striking the boat broadside and throwing them sideways. Rygal was thrown against the rail, and in the same second the fish in his net, as if sensing his hold loosen, gave a mighty heave away from the boat.

It happened so fast Rygal didn't have time to even take a breath—the next thing he knew, he was in the water, freezing cold salt water. The shock of the cold took his breath away. Something was around his right wrist, biting into his arm—he realized, in a second of horror, that it was the net. Somehow, he had become entangled, and now the fish were pulling away furiously, much stronger than he was in the water.

He surfaced, coughing, the burning cold of the saltwater stinging his throat. "Norrin!" he cried out, the words muffled as another wave hit him in the face. He saw Norrin at the oars again, saw him bring the boat around sharply—

The fish heaved forward again, and he was dragged under, the threads of the net digging into his arm. Panic gripped him. Something was wrong—the fish were pulling with far too much strength for such a small catch. Then he realized why. He had been pulled back into the current, and was now being carried east by the roiling waves.

"Norrin!" he screamed again, eyes blurred by salt water, making it nearly impossible to see. He heard Norrin shouting his name, and flailed desperately towards him—another wave hit him in the face, submerging him again, and he came up gasping for air. He was a strong swimmer, but this water was unlike any he had swam in before—this was a roiling, clutching beast, this sea.

"Go with the current!" Norrin's voice came faintly to his ears. "Let it carry you! Don't fight it or it will drown you—let it carry you!"

Rygal coughed frantically, but stopped flailing, realizing Norrin was right.

"Norrin," he called again, this time in wretched defeat. The waves heaved around him, roiling and rocking him—the net tightened around his wrist, forcing him under again.

He fought back to the surface in time to watch the waves carry the skiff out of sight—he tried to scream again, but the water filled his mouth and he could only cough. Over the waves came Norrin's voice, tight with desperation. "I'll find you, Rygal! I'll find you!"

"Norrin!" Rygal cried once more, and then he was pulled under again. The strength of the current was horrific. The waves, tugging him from side to side, left him helpless, utterly powerless in the grip of the sea.

Something bumped into him—he managed to reach out and grasp it, forcing his head up out of the water, as the current dragged him on.

. . . . . .

It was the gritty taste of sand in his teeth that pulled him out of the semi-consciousness that he had sunk into. He slumped, his head on the beam of driftwood that had bumped into him and, in a way, saved his life. A few strands from the net were still wrapped tightly around his arm—the fish must have pulled themselves free. Sand had been washed into his face by the waves—sand, sand from a beach—

His eyes flew open, and he raised his head. He was ten feet or so from the beach—he could see the dark outlines of trees and the sinking sun lighting the sand.

It didn't matter if it was an unknown beach, Rygal decided in a second, he had to get out of the freezing water. He let go of the driftwood and half-swam half-crawled to shore. The wind bit into him in another moment, making him shiver—he crashed down on the sand, shivering, his head aching, his throat still burning from the saltwater. He coughed until he was sure there was no more sea water inside him.

"Norrin," he called weakly, his voice rasping. There was no reply; if Norrin had made it out of the storm, then he would have kept following the current, until he found Rygal—or would he have gone back to Gayrile, to get help from the other sailors? Rygal wasn't sure, but he sensed, with a cold finality, that it would be a long while before he was found.

*Where am I?*

He looked up, surveying his surroundings, and tried to think. The sun was sinking slowly in the west—Norrin had said the current traveled east, and Rygal had been carried by it for hours—and that meant he was on the Mainland.

The realization would have been more exciting had he not been soaking wet, alone, still sore from the fight with the soldiers, and only wearing his shirt and breeches. He got up and paced the beach for a little while, searching for any signs of life and for his belongings. He found one of his boots, which served little use, so he tossed it away again.

He had no idea of where he was specifically, but he could no longer stand the cold. Norrin had showed him how to make a fire from wood being rubbed together very fast—friction force, he called it. Rygal moved a little ways from the beach, just within the tree line, and collected tinder and branches.

If he had gone east, that meant he was likely farther from home than he had first thought—the country east of Coonsia was a blur in his mind, and in the cold and exhaustion his thoughts moved slowly. He rubbed two sticks together in silence for what felt like a long time, producing only thin strands of smoke, until his eyes picked out the tiny speck of light from the sparks.

He added more tinder and blew, making the smoke billow all the more, until flames finally flickered to life inside the pile. In the same moment, the images of Norrin's maps of the world came back in a flash, and he looked up triumphantly. "Daffodalion," he murmured.

And immediately despair set in again. *Daffodalion?* Daffodalion was a country of mystery and wilderness, of strange creatures and wild things. It was miles from Gayrile. Not only that, the country was huge. There was no telling where exactly he was, or how far the current had swept him.

Perhaps he could get west to Coonsia, to Caer Sia, even. Perhaps…

A twig snapped behind him, and he jumped up, moving closer to the warmth and light of the fire. In the same moment, he realized how exposed he was here. Who knew what creatures lurked in these woods, or if they were particularly hungry…

A figure appeared in the shadows. Not a tall figure, shorter than he was, slightly built. He saw the stranger edging forward slowly, hesitantly, then crouch in the bracken, almost invisible. He thought he could see the shadow of a large dog behind the stranger.

"Who's there?" he demanded with as much courage as he could muster.

The voice that replied startled him—it was not a threatening tone, nor was it a beast's growl. The voice was soft, curious, and—most surprising—a girl's voice.

"Hello—could we get warm for a minute, please?"

# 3

## The Runaways

*A girl?* Rygal was totally confused by the voice. What was a girl doing in woods like these? Besides that, she sounded young—quite young, probably younger than he was, so what was she doing out here?

"Who are you?" he finally asked slowly, peering through the shadows. In the half-light, and with the uncertain flicker of firelight, he could only see a dark outline of the strange girl, crouched in the bracken.

There was the low, uneasy growl from a dog behind the girl, and Rygal stepped back quickly.

"Settle down, Tag," came the girl's voice again. Rygal could see her patting a large and very shaggy dog. "We're not going to hurt you, human—we're just cold."

"Well… come closer, then," Rygal said finally. His brain hinged on one thing the girl had said—she had called him "human," and that was odd…

The girl stood and moved into the firelight. There was a rustling behind her as the dog followed. It was a wolfhound, still quite young, Rygal noticed—and now that it had been reassured there was no danger, its tail was wagging in a slow, cheerful rhythm.

His attention was drawn back to the girl, who was slowly coming into focus as she moved to the fire. Bright green eyes—not gray-green, like a human's green, but deep green, like the forest. Rygal had never seen someone with eyes like that. Her face was young—she was probably only around ten or eleven, younger than he was. Her hair, long and dark, fell in ringlets down past her shoulders. It was probably very pretty hair if it wasn't filled with tangles and bits of thorns, which it was now.

As she warmed herself by the fire, the light illuminated her form, and Rygal stared in both wonder and confusion. While he had taken the girl to be wearing a coat made of furs, he now realized, to his bewilderment, that the fur was her own—a thick pelt of soft black fur that covered her torso and mid-leg. He also could see, now that the light was better, her upturned nose, pointed ears, a face that was not quite human—

She *wasn't* human.

"You're a… Wildkid," he said at last, searching for the word. The name was one from stories, from myths and legends that the old women would tell back home, one that was attached to the young children who liked playing in the mud—"little wildkid," their parents would chuckle…

"I didn't know you were real," he added finally, as the girl had hardly reacted to his statement.

Now she looked up at him, a quizzical expression on her face.

"I didn't know humans were real, either. I'd never seen one before this week." She looked him up and down critically. "You're a little smaller than the others."

"I'm only twelve!" Rygal protested. "I'll grow."

She seemed to consider this, then smiled and nodded. "Well, it can't be helped anyway. I like the size you are—if you were taller you would be scarier. Like the traders."

Rygal looked up, suddenly hopeful. "Traders? You mean there's a port nearby?" If the traders were still here, maybe he could go with them—maybe they could take him home—

"No port, as far as I know," the Wildkid girl said. "There were traders that came to Kasabren a few weeks ago. We did business with them. I wanted a look inside their ships, and then they kidnapped me." Her face had fallen. "I don't know why."

"Well, you're a Wildkid—they could—" Rygal stopped himself. It wouldn't do much good to explain to her that a real, living Wildkid would probably gain much profit as a circus sideshow or something along those lines.

"You look very tired. You should sleep. Tag and I can keep watch," the girl said, standing and stretching. "And then we can decide what to do tomorrow."

"We… what?" Rygal said, confused. He was tired and sore—this made it harder to think things through. But if he didn't have to stay up, looking out for danger… if he had this strange new companion…

"I'll be back. Tag will stay with you." She disappeared into the woods again.

"I… wait…" Rygal started, then stopped and yawned. The adrenaline of earlier was wearing on him, and now he felt exhausted.

Still confused and a little fearful, he curled up close to the fire, the flicker of the flames and the warmth eventually lulling him to sleep.

......

Rygal woke to the strange cries of the birds. Dazed and disoriented for an instant, he tried to remember what had happened and where he was. Then he remembered the storm, being dragged into the sea, and now he was here, with…

He looked around. The Wildkid girl was nowhere to be seen; the wolfhound, Tag, was still asleep across the clearing. The fire was dying down, and now in the chill morning air, with his damp clothes, Rygal was freezing. He got up and found a few fallen branches to add to the fire, then settled down beside it again and thought for a long moment.

He was alone in an unknown land with no cloak, no shoes, and no other provisions. He was hungry and quite thirsty. And now there was a young Wildkid girl here too, somehow…

There was a soft rustling in the brush to his left, and he turned swiftly. It was only the girl, carrying something on a piece of bark.

"Hello—I'm glad to see you're awake. I was looking for food."

"Did you find any?" Rygal asked.

She held out the bark, which carried three small fish. "Not much, sorry. But I guess it's something."

"It's better than nothing," Rygal told her, feeling a small surge of hope, and looked at her again. "You can hunt? And fish?" He knew Wildkids were some of the best natural hunters in the world, which meant that maybe this girl could be very helpful.

She shrugged slightly. "Not very well—not like the others in my Clan. But I can do it a little."

"That's great. That's perfect." Rygal stoked the fire, creating a small space in the coals to cook the fish in. "Okay... might work better to cut them up, and roast them on spits. Can you go cut a few green branches? Then they won't burn."

The girl got up and disappeared for a little while. By the time she returned, carrying the sticks, Rygal had cleaned and gutted the fish by the sea. It was messy work, considering the only tool he had was a sharp stone. But it was better than nothing, as they'd pointed out before.

They speared the pieces of fish on the sticks and set them over the fire, then both sat in silence.

"So... you were taken by traders?" Rygal asked finally, for the sake of conversation.

"Yes. They were there to do business with my father, the chieftain of the Mara-N'Tell."

"Is that your... tribe?"

"Clan. There's five of them," she explained matter-of-factly. "Mara-N'Tell, Mara-Syan, Mara-Yefridi, Mara-Rinla, and Mara-D'Brenna."

The foreign words were unfamiliar to Rygal, but he found the story fascinating. "Well… what do I call you, anyway?"

The Wildkid girl stood, straightened, and bowed slightly in the fashion of her people, touching her fingers to her lips, brow, and then chest. "I am Dusty, daughter of Tyslip, daughter of Connira. First born of Chief Sorrel."

Rygal looked at her, impressed. "Your father is the chief?"

Dusty nodded proudly, then looked at him quizzically. "And what's your name?"

"I'm Rygal, son of Maran. Of Gayrile."

Dusty thought a moment. "I don't know where Gayrile is. I've heard of it, I think, but I've never been to the Mainland before."

"Me neither, honestly," Rygal admitted with a faint grin. "Well, Gayrile is north of here—it's one of the Northern Isles. By my guesses we're in Daffodalion."

There was a brief pause. Dusty settled down by the fire, her brow furrowed. "What are you going to do?"

Rygal thought a moment, realizing he still had to come up with a plan. "I'm not sure. Caer Sia might be our best bet. But if Norrin's right… I'm not sure that'd be safe."

"Who is Norrin?" Dusty asked. "And why not?"

Rygal took a breath, not sure he should tell her. Then he shrugged mentally. She was here with him, so she might as well know the risks. "Well, Norrin says—he's my guardian, by the way—he says that there's trouble in Coonsia. Gayrile's had a lot of problems in the last few years, most of them brought about by someone named Safacon. And now this Safacon has sent his deputy Kado to attack Caer Sia."

"Why?"

"Well, Caer Sia is the only thing keeping Safacon from taking over Gayrile already," Rygal explained. "I mean—since Gayrile is ultimately under the High King, Safacon's had to keep his conquest on the down low up till now. But now he's done with that—now he's ready to attack."

Dusty looked interested. "So it might not be safe to go to this Caer Sia place? Even though that's where the Liznee people are?"

"Right… and they might be able to help us. At the very least there's a port there, so I can go home."

The fish had seared to a lovely black color, and the smell of cooking meat rose in the air. Dusty removed them from the spits, setting them back on the bark. She and Rygal ate the pieces in silence. Aside from the numerous small bones, the fish weren't bad, and Rygal was hungry enough to take whatever he could have. By the time they finished, his mouth felt dry from want of water.

"We're going to have to find water soon," he said, standing.

Dusty was feeding Tag the leftover fish. "Well, we're along the coast. If we follow the coastline west, towards Caer Sia, then we'll eventually find a stream soon, and then we can follow it back to the spring."

"Right," Rygal murmured. He doused the fire, covering it with sand, then turned to his two companions. There was a level of responsibility here, he realized, leading a young Wildkid to Caer Sia. He felt it settle on him. He decided, then and there, that he would be sure nothing happened to either Dusty or Tag. He had to keep them safe.

He looked towards the trees. "All right, well, let's go."

. . . . . .

They followed the coastline for a while, keeping just within the trees. Rygal had never seen woods like these. The forests along Gayrile's coast were spindly and stunted by sea wind and weather. These trees were taller than two houses, towering up as far as he could see, their great boughs stretching over them.

After twenty minutes or so the beach became rocky and treacherous, and they were forced to turn and walk in the forest. They had still seen no sign of fresh water. Rygal's mouth was dry, and his stomach was beginning to cramp.

Dusty moved on ahead, taking it all in. Her fur mottled with the shadows of the trees, so at times she was almost invisible. At one point she vanished around a bend.

Rygal jogged ahead, pricking his feet on the branches and needles on the ground, looking around for her. "Hey!" he called finally, panicking for an instant that he had been left alone.

Dusty appeared in another second from the bushes to his right. "Come here—I found something."

Rygal shook his head in both relief and frustration that she'd made him worry. "We don't have time for exploring, Dusty—"

"I found water," Dusty interrupted, raising an eyebrow.

Rygal stopped, feeling guilty. "You did? Where?"

He followed her through the brush, up a small hill, into a meadow. The grass grew tall and green, waving in the wind. He could see a rocky outcrop ahead and could hear the water trickling off it.

They pushed through the grass and stood in a clearing. Several dogwood trees grew in a circle around a spring. Water bubbled up through the rocks, washing down in a stream. Tag was already lapping it up greedily, his tail wagging.

Rygal and Dusty ran forward and took turns drinking the fresh water. The taste of clean water washed away the lingering stinging salt in Rygal's throat, and he felt much refreshed after he finished. He leaned back against the rocks, surveying the scene. "That's odd," he said after a while. "It's nearly winter… dogwood trees shouldn't be blooming…"

"Can't you feel it?" Dusty asked, her voice filled with awe. "Those kind of rules don't apply to this place. This place—this must be the Forest of Light. My father has told me about it several times, but it's been a long time since any Wildkid set foot here."

Rygal looked around, a little unsure. "What is it?"

"It's… well, it's a place of refuge. Created at the dawn of time, after evil entered the world. A place that no evil could ever touch. No war, no death. The High Light created it after the Dividing War, I think."

Rygal looked around. This place certainly fit the description of the wood that he had long since dismissed as mythology. The entire place seemed to breathe with life, like one living creature. Birds twittered cheerily in the trees, and butterflies flitted about the flowers. There was peace here, calm. They seemed suspended in the glory of the silent wood. Norrin had told him the story of the Making, and Rygal thought he remembered something about the Forest of Light…

He had dismissed most of it as mere mythology, but here they were. Perhaps the rest of it was true too.

They didn't have any way to store the water from the spring, so the best they could do was drink their fill and keep moving. They walked for several minutes in the wood, the light and life of the Forest letting Rygal know that they were still in the same place. He sensed when they left a few moments later, entering the shadowed woods again.

"I can hear people," Dusty said unexpectedly.

Rygal turned sharply. The sleepiness and peace of the Forest of Light had somehow made him forget their predicament. He also remembered, with a jolt, what Norrin had told him of Kado.

"You do? Where?" He strained his ears, but could hear nothing. Dusty looked around slowly, her green eyes scanning the wood.

The fur along her back had stood up, like an uneasy cat. "I—I don't know—but I can hear them moving through the woods. I think they're a distance away still."

"Probably… otherwise I'd be able to hear them too," Rygal decided slowly.

"I don't think you would," Dusty said softly.

Her matter-of-fact tone rankled him somehow. "And why's that?"

Dusty looked at him and shrugged slightly, and her answer chilled him to the core. "Because they aren't breathing."

*Kado.* Rygal swung around, looking swiftly around the shadowed wood, remembering what Norrin had told him of the deathless host. He could hear nothing but the distant cry of birdsong, the rustle of the wind through the ferns—all normal sounds. But the silence was sinister.

"Run," he whispered finally. "Down the hill into the ravine—we can hide there—"

They jogged through the brush. Dusty moved slower, still turning and looking around—Rygal could see her face registering the many sounds and scents that he couldn't pick up.

"Faster," Rygal urged her. Dusty had paused uncertainly, listening intently.

"Hang on—I can hear something else—someone below us—"

"I don't hear anything—let's go." Rygal grabbed her arm, and together they ran down the slope into the ravine. Tag trotted behind them, his ears flicked back, his tail curled up in alert.

They reached the base of the ridge and stood for several moments, panting, listening for several tense seconds. Dusty was silent, her eyes still flicking around them uneasily.

"Hear anything now?" Rygal asked.

The words were barely out of his mouth when the tell-tale clatter of horse hooves came from down the ravine path.

# 4

A Tale of Two Wanderers

Rygal stood frozen in fear for a moment, unable to move. His mind went rapidly to thoughts of Kado, and remembered all that Norrin had told him. They were trapped—there was no way they could outrun such a force.

In a second, he made his decision.

"Run," he panted hoarsely to Dusty. "Along the ravine—go as fast as you can."

Dusty looked at him, her young face worried. "What are you going to do?"

"I'll hold them off," Rygal said, trying to sound brave, but his voice trembled.

Dusty considered this for a moment, then shrugged slowly. "Wouldn't it be better if we both did that?"

Rygal opened his mouth to argue, then realized that as much as he would like to think otherwise, he was terrified at the thought of being left here alone. He wasn't sure how much help Dusty could offer… but still, it was better than nothing. "Do you think they'll capture us?"

She glanced at him, a slight frown on her face. "They aren't the ones I heard in the wood. These ones are breathing."

That meant it wasn't Kado's undead force coming for them now. That thought somehow made Rygal relax. "How many?" he asked as they edged along the boulders, seeking for a hiding place.

Dusty peeked over the rocks, peering down the path. The thin road curved slightly around the sheer cliff they huddled beside, which made it impossible to see who was coming. "I don't know— but not a whole army." Her voice was more puzzled than scared.

"Get down," Rygal cautioned her, pulling her into the shadow of the rocks. Tag sat beside him, ears flicked forward, his hackles raised in uncertainty. "Good boy," Rygal murmured to the young wolfhound, who wagged his tail slightly but made no other move.

The horses were drawing nearer—Rygal could hear the animals panting, snorting as they jogged along. He pressed himself back against the rock that Dusty hid behind, but couldn't quite get the rest of himself behind the boulder, and so he had a clear view of the road.

Two horses, a bay and a black, clip-clopped into view, moving at a brisk trot. Their riders seemed engaged in conversation—one huge and muscular, with a green cloak, the other tall and lean, wearing a mottled gray cloak.

Rygal didn't move, hardly dared to breathe as they approached.

They were just passing him when the rider on the black horse turned his head, his keen green eyes locking on Rygal. Rygal saw confusion—then suspicion—cross his face.

He reined in sharply. His companion, who was still talking, turned in confusion, then frowned as he saw Rygal.

Rygal remained frozen against the wall, heart pounding, totally unsure of what to say.

"Who are you?" the rider on the black horse asked. His voice was clear and crisp, with an elegant Northern accent punctuating the vowels in the words.

Rygal stepped away from the rocks, pushing Tag behind him, stammering for a reply. "I—I'm no one, sir, I think I'm lost…"

He saw the stranger's face soften. "Forgive me. I don't believe you to be a foe. At least not yet." There was a tiny hint of humor in the stranger's green eyes. He was tall and wiry, with whipcord strength. He had no hair on his head or face, and his skin was silver. Those features marked him as a Liznee. Over his right eye was a scar that trailed down to his jaw.

Rygal was certain he had seen this stranger before…in a book, perhaps? He wasn't sure. The other rider was unfamiliar, with a scruffy dark beard. There was probably at least one drop of giant's blood in his veins, Rygal decided, judging by his size alone—the man was easily twice his height.

"I say, yer honor, looks like we've found someone," the giant announced loudly.

"I would say we have," said the Liznee, studying Rygal carefully. Finally he straightened. "Who are you, boy? And what are you doing in these lands?"

"I'm—Rygal. Son of Maran. Of Gayrile," Rygal said slowly, trying to sound older.

"Gayrile?" the giant echoed, glancing at the other rider.

The Liznee's face was unchanged, but Rygal could see suspicion in his eyes, and suddenly felt a prickle of fear. "What part of Gayrile?" he asked slowly, dismounting and moving forward.

A small stone struck the rock behind him, a few feet from his head. "Stop!" Dusty's voice rang over the scene. She crouched on top of a boulder ten paces from them, holding a second rock, larger than the first, at the ready. "He's with me—don't hurt him or I'll crush your head."

Rygal looked at her in horror, then back at the stranger, sure the Liznee would kill them both.

A slight smile was playing at the Liznee's face. "I believe you," he said mildly. Dusty lowered the stone slightly, still looking unsure— below her, at the base of the rock, Tag was growling warily.

The Liznee looked back at Rygal. "I mean no threat to either of you, and I am only asking questions. Strange rumors have come from Gayrile as of late, and so we are trying to sort them all out."

"What sort of rumors?" Rygal asked, as Dusty slid down from the rock and trotted over.

"Nothing good," the Liznee replied grimly. He shook his head. "They will be solved eventually, I am sure. In the meantime, what are you two doing out in these wilds?"

"We—well, we aren't sure where we are," Rygal said slowly.

"Dusty was taken by traders and I was swept here in a storm—now we're farther from the coast than we wanted to be and we still don't know where we are."

"We're trying to get to Caer Sia," Dusty piped up.

"Are you indeed. Well then, it might be best for you to stay with us. We ride for Caer Sia with important news."

Rygal nodded, feeling quite relieved, then looked up curiously. "Then—who are you?"

"My companion is Glentree, my deputy and friend," the Liznee said, nodding to the giant. He extended a hand. "I am Dandio Ki."

He said it calmly, but Rygal stepped back, stunned for an instant. "What… you… you are Dandio?" he gasped finally. Dandio Ki, Commander of the Red Dawn, brother of the High King—and Rygal had behaved so rudely to him—

"Yes, I am," Dandio said with the same half-smile. He was still holding out a hand, waiting.

Rygal couldn't bring himself to take it. He was totally at a loss as to how to address such a hero. Finally he dropped to one knee, motioning for Dusty to do the same. "Sir—I didn't know—"

"None of that!" Dandio said hastily, helping him up again. "Honestly, I was never one for all that protocol. Ĵan was, but never me." He smiled slightly. "That's why he's the king and I'm the commander."

Hearing such a thing made Rygal smile weakly, and he finally shook Dandio's hand in greeting. "Then… is the Red Dawn near here too? What are you doing here?"

Dandio shook his head. "Our army remains at Caer Sia. Glentree and I are traveling back from the eastern cities—we spoke with their barons."

"An' we'll no doubt find your company more agreeable than theirs," Glentree added with a crooked grin.

"What did you mean about rumor from Gayrile? Is it about the warlord? About… Kado?" Rygal asked slowly.

The two riders exchanged a glance. "It seems you know of what we face," Dandio commented at last.

"Just a little," Rygal said.

"We heard people while we were up there," Dusty said, pointing up the hill towards the forest. "Well, I did—but it sounded odd, not at all normal…"

A shadow crossed Dandio's face as Dusty spoke, and his expression was suddenly serious. "Come with us. We had best discuss these things after we make camp." He lifted Dusty up behind Glentree, and swung into the saddle. "Come along, Rygal of Gayrile—we have much to discuss."

Still in a daze, Rygal mounted up behind Dandio, and they clattered on down the path.

. . . . . .

They rode for an hour or so, gradually moving west, Tag trotting along behind the horses. As the sun began to dip down behind the trees, Dandio called a halt, and they set up camp in a small clearing surrounded by thickets.

Glentree and Dandio traveled light, Rygal realized. Glentree unloaded the gear, setting it in a neat pile, and then set to building a fire. Dandio offered Rygal a pair of boots, which while a little too big, protected his bruised feet.

Rygal and Dusty stood in the background, not quite sure how to help. Dandio seemed to notice and had Dusty help Glentree gather more wood, while he and Rygal prepared the evening meal.

"Nothing much," the Liznee commented as he rummaged through the bags. "We've got a fire, that's good—hot dinner is more appealing in the cold evenings."

Rygal nodded, his stomach tight with hunger. Aside from the two little fish that morning, he hadn't eaten all day. "I never pictured… well, a Commanding General… having to cook meals," he admitted finally.

"Glentree normally offers," Dandio said. "He says it's out of duty, but he only offered after the first time we were on the trail." He chuckled softly to himself, then looked back at the other bags. "Pull out that pot in there, and a few water flasks—we killed a rabbit this morning before running into you two, and the meat will taste excellent in a soup."

Rygal did as instructed. He was still a little in awe of who was talking to him, but he was beginning to relax. There was a calm, easy-going air about the Liznee that made him feel calmer too. "Sir—Dandio—earlier today, Dusty and I got water in a forest—a different kind of forest than the rest of this place."

Dandio nodded. "The Forest of Light. A haven for peace and life. Created by the High Light Himself after the Dividing War, or so the legends say."

"The Dividing War?"

"Long ago, there was a battle between the species. Many lives were lost, and this part of the world has never been the same, so they say."

"Why did they fight?" Rygal asked, fascinated by the story.

Dandio smiled wryly as he set the pot over the fire. "Well, the legend says that the Netrocrians and the Fyrocrians always despised one another, and so they battled, but I'm not sure how much of that is true, or why they hated each other."

"The...who...?"

"That's a story for another time," Dandio told him, shaking his head, but he was smiling. "You will drain me entirely with all your questions."

Glentree stoked the fire, and they settled down to wait while the soup cooked.

"Well then, young'uns," Glentree rumbled as he sat down heavily. "Let's have your story, then. I'm most interested to hear it."

Rygal glanced at Dusty, then shrugged slightly. "Well, her side of the story comes first."

Dusty nodded and began. "I got here the day before we met Rygal. My Clan had gone to the coast, to meet with traders from

Drynrall Island. They exchanged goods with us and made ready to leave. One of them asked if I wanted to go on board, since their ships were so different than ours. I did—my papa didn't see me go, no one did." She looked down at her hands, her face sad and worried. "They locked me up right away. Tag followed me, I didn't know he did. They got him too." Tag settled down next to her, his ears flicked back, as if understanding the story.

Dandio and Glentree looked grim. Glentree shook his head, his face scornful. "Those Drynrall traders are just as much pirates—no wonder they'd want to take ya. We're glad you got away," he added, smiling at her.

"How *did* you get away?" Rygal asked. He hadn't heard this much of the story yet.

Dusty smiled slightly. "We sailed north for three weeks, I think—though I lost track of time below decks. We went north up the Durbin Strait and then west towards Coonsia. I think they planned to sell their wares in Kilee."

"It's probably the right guess," Dandio told her.

"Yes, well, they docked off shore. I got Tag loose and we got away. We were in the woods that first night, and the next night we found Rygal's fire."

Silence fell for several moments. Darkness and chill had settled over the forest, yet here by the fire, it was comforting and warm.

"And what about you, lad?" Glentree asked finally, looking at Rygal.

Rygal could feel the eyes of the others on him, and shrugged slightly. "It's not as interesting as hers. I was fishing off the coast of Gayrile with my guardian, Norrin—we got caught in a storm."

"Norrin?" Dandio repeated, raising his head. "So he's still all right, after all these years?"

Rygal stared at him in surprise. "You know him?" Norrin, shabby fisherman Norrin—a friend of Dandio Ki—

"Not as well as you, I'm sure," Dandio admitted with a slight smile. "But a few of our people helped found the Guardians of Gayrile with him." He looked up. "He's your mentor?"

"Yeah—we were fishing, I caught something in my net, but the storm picked up—I got washed overboard and tangled up, and then swept east by the Current." Rygal turned back to Dandio, still caught up on the Norrin bit. "I didn't know he helped found the Guardians… I thought he just fought with them."

"I doubt he'd want you to know too much, so it would do little good discussing it with him now," Dandio said. "It was his idea, his and a few Liznees, like I said. They did it together."

The news was stunning, and Rygal could barely believe it. Norrin, one of the founders of the Guardians of Gayrile—

"What happened to them?" Dusty asked softly, looking up at Dandio. "I have only heard a little of the Guardians, and they sounded unstoppable."

Dandio took a heavy breath. "About a decade ago, after the fall of the tyrannical queen Kircadash, a man named Safacon rose in power in Gayrile. He had great power in alchemy, and in the ancient Wizard arts, much like Norrin did."

"Norrin?" Rygal echoed, even more startled. "He was a…"

"A wizard. A powerful one too. I am afraid after the Guardians were defeated, he kept his powers hidden away for fear of causing any more of his comrades to die."

Rygal looked away, shocked by this revelation. Norrin had not been a simple warrior in the Guardians—he had been their leader.

And Safacon had forced him into hiding, and killed many of his fellow warriors. Along with Maran. He stared at the ground.

"I didn't know any of that," he said at last, somehow feeling cheated.

"He probably doesn't like to talk about it now. I wouldn't either, if I was in his place." Dandio took a breath. "But with the situation in Gayrile now, I'm glad to hear he's doing well."

"You mean… with Safacon?" Rygal guessed.

Dandio nodded gravely. "Safacon has, as of late, broken all ties with Caer Sia. He has rebelled, unofficially, as it were. I fear it may be a long time before Gayrile is safe again."

"Norrin says Kado is working with Safacon," Rygal said. "He said that Kado is his deputy—and that he has…" he trailed off, not sure how to put it. The idea of an army of undead was the stuff of legends, and it felt almost silly to talk about it here.

But Dandio was looking at him and nodding slowly. "Norrin is right, in that sense. Safacon has always been interested in alchemy and working magic—with the Objects of Power that he created, he can do virtually anything. Kado is another matter. Kado's focus is not in a sizable force, as Safacon's is, but in the quality of his warriors. That is why Kado has taken quite a while studying and learning until he could create the Hazes."

"Hazes?" Dusty asked softly. "What are Hazes?"

Dandio and Glentree exchanged a quick glance. "It's not a night time tale, you two," Glentree said at last. "We'll tell ya a bit of it, at least, just so's you know. Kado had several men in his army volunteer for an experiment, and he concocted some sort of cauldron in which he created them. That made the Hazes."

"What do they… do?" Rygal asked.

Dandio took a breath. "Well, to put it lightly, that spell makes them immortal—deathless to everything, or so we've gathered. They have caused considerable damage already. Not only that, those Hazes—they're very strong, much stronger than a normal man. And they're…changed, in another way. They don't remember anything about their past lives—they're just there. I couldn't call it life."

"The spell enhances anything about the victims that was already there," Glentree explained. "So if you got a real skilled warrior, he'll be an extra skilled Haze. The Hazes—they're shells, husks of the former people they were. All Kado's done is taken the worst parts inside a man and amplified it."

"Then… they can't be stopped," Rygal said with a horrible sinking feeling.

"There is a way," Dandio said, his eyes two green lights of flame. "And we will figure it out. There's always a catch with spells like these, and Kado was especially hasty in creating them—that means there has to be some weakness the Hazes have that we haven't yet learned."

"What could it be?" Dusty asked slowly. She sat huddled by the fire, stroking Tag's shaggy fur.

"That's what we don't yet know," Dandio admitted.

"But don't think we'll give up," Glentree boomed. "The Star people never abandoned hope, back in the ancient battles."

"The Stars," Dandio said. "No, they never did. But we must win this battle without them, I fear."

"The Stars," Dusty echoed, her eyes shining as she stared up into the sky. "The ancient warriors of the night sky." Her eyes traced the shimmering constellation of the Northern Sword. "What I love about them most, I think, is you could be anywhere on Orlell and you could still look up and see that same sword."

Rygal studied the sky. Strange, he thought vaguely, how the longer you look at stars, the more seemed to appear. "Norrin would tell me the stories of the Seven Servants of the High Light," he said softly. "They are the most powerful of the Star people, and they do the bidding of the High Light, sometimes even bringing His messages down to Orlell." He paused. "Is the High Light real, Dandio? I mean, no one but the Stars have even seen Him."

Dandio was silent for a moment. "Is the wind real? You can feel it—see its works—watch it tear down. But no one has ever seen it." He smiled slightly. "That's the way of the High Light—we've never seen Him, but we've seen His works." He looked back at the sky. "Even if the Forest of Light is the only remnant of His glory left here, we must still seek His promises."

There was a long silence. The wind stirred the trees, blowing across Rygal's face.

Dandio finally stood. "Well, you'd best have some dinner before sleep. Glentree, I'll take the first watch. Perhaps we can loan our new friends those extra sleeping mats for the night."

"Aye, sir," Glentree said, moving to the horses and returning with two sleeping mats as well as two blankets. "It'll be a little chilly," he told them as they spread the mats out. "Best set 'em by the fire an' you'll stay nice an' warm."

Rygal settled down by the fire with a warm bowl of rabbit stew. Despite the chill weather, having a mat under him and a blanket over him was such a welcome change from last night that he didn't mind. He curled up, staring into the flames, deep in thought until he slipped off to sleep.

Partway through the night, he dreamed of Hazes wreaking havoc on Caer Sia and marching towards Gayrile. Fearfully, he tried to stop them, but he couldn't. He fought desperately, but each move seemed to be in vain. Panic filled him, and he hung between despair and sorrow. Then—maybe in his dream, perhaps in reality—a wind brushed across his face, cool and calming.

*Be still.*

He heard the voice, and wondered if it had been within his dream or not.

Before he could think about it, he had fallen back asleep.

# 5

The Voice of Kado

Birdsong woke Rygal, drawing him out of sleep. He was still curled up beside the fire. Tag slept beside him; Rygal patted the shaggy wolfhound, who wagged his tail softly.

"Good morning," came Dusty's voice. She sat across from him on the other side of the fire.

"Morning," Rygal said groggily, rubbing his eyes. He sat up and looked around. Glentree was tending the horses, but there was no sign of their leader. "Where's Dandio?"

"Mornin', lad—he's gone back towards the Forest of Light to get water, but I'll bet he'll be back in a bit. He wanted to investigate what Dusty heard yesterday," the giant told him. He removed one of the saddlebags and started towards the fire. "Breakfast is almost ready."

Rygal rolled up his mat and settled down by the fire, trying to warm his feet. By now his bare feet were scratched and bruised, covered with dirt. He figured the rest of him looked like that too. The bruises and cuts from the incident with the soldiers were only a fraction of the many small injuries scoring his body.

The pot of water over the fire rose to a boil, and Glentree offered both the children tea. He got to work with a skillet of eggs and potatoes, and in another moment breakfast was ready.

Rygal ate hungrily, grateful for the second warm meal in the last twenty-four hours. He accepted a second mug of tea, and looked up at Glentree. "Where will we go today?"

"We'll keep moving west. We've got a lot of ground to cover a' fore we cross the border, and even then we'll have to go quick—the mountain passes will be blocked with snow sooner than you'd think."

"What would we do if they were blocked?" Dusty asked.

"We'd go the long way, around the mountains to Badwater, and then east by sea. Ideally we won't have to do that. Speed is our friend at the moment—we need to get to Caer Sia before Kado does. The High King is counting on us." Glentree finished his breakfast, rinsed off the plates, and put the cooking items back in the saddlebags. "Better get packed up—time to get going."

Rygal helped him repack the saddlebags and fasten them back on behind the horse's saddle. Glentree instructed him to grab the kettle, which they had left by the fire along with Dandio's share of breakfast for when he returned.

Rygal moved to obey, and at the same moment a shrill, wailing noise rose up from the woods.

Glentree's head snapped up at the sound. "That's Dandio's hunting horn," he said, almost to himself. "Something's amiss."

The horn sounded once again, then all was quiet. Even the birds had fallen silent. The forest was suddenly still.

"Get 'ere," Glentree ordered, and both children crossed quickly to him.

Rygal's heart pounded with fear. Something was wrong—he sensed it. The birds hadn't gone quiet at Dandio's horn, he was sure of that. Something else, something worse, was wrong.

Glentree lifted Dusty up onto the horse and reached for Rygal, who stepped back.

"I can fight. I can help you," he insisted. He hated the thought of being sent away on horseback and leaving Glentree and Dandio to face off against unknown foes.

"No time for that, young'un, right now you got to follow orders," Glentree told him, but he turned swiftly at the sound of horse hooves.

Dandio's sleek black mare cantered into the glade. Dandio hardly waited for the horse to stop as he slid from her back, and faced his comrades. "Get the gear. Mount up. Hurry!"

"What's—?" Glentree started.

Dandio had lifted the remaining saddlebags onto his horse and paused only long enough to reply. "Hazes!"

Rygal's throat felt dry. "Here?" he asked shakily.

"Coming," Dandio corrected, as Glentree finished gathering the supplies. "That's why we're leaving. Now, while we can."

"But…can't you fight them?" Rygal asked, a little of his fear leaving him. Dandio and Glentree were both skilled warriors—surely they could fight.

Dandio smiled slightly. "I appreciate the compliment, but I definitely couldn't beat them. Not alone. And we can't afford to have them catch us."

Tag snarled unexpectedly, his eyes riveted on the far edge of the glade. Rygal didn't hear anything, but he trusted the wolf's senses. He tried one more time. "But—but Dandio, couldn't I fight too? I'm sure I could try to—"

"Not here," Dandio said shortly. He looked at him hard. "This is not the place. Right now we've got to go—we've got to go now, before they—"

But he was cut off as the brush at the far end of the glade was flung aside, and three figures stepped towards them.

"Go!" Dandio barked. Glentree mounted up in front of Dusty, snapped the reins, and galloped away. Tag stood uneasily, growling, but the sight of the attackers and a whistle from Dusty sent him bounding in retreat. Rygal started towards Dandio's horse, but stopped, unable to tear his eyes away from the—things—in the clearing right now.

He hadn't expected Hazes to look anything like this—in his mind, he'd imagined tall, muscular figures clad in black, or maybe ghostlike wraiths with swords. The creatures were certainly tall, and very muscular, but their builds were bizarre. They all looked like they'd been human, once upon a time, but what they'd become was utterly alien. Their bodies were human enough, but the picture was incomplete, as though they'd been broken and then pieced together incorrectly. Rygal was reminded of an image someone had drawn in the sand, with the fuzzy, blurred lines forming the body. Their skin was gray—not the handsome silver tone that Dandio's was, but dulled, deadened gray. Like a corpse's skin. And the faces were the worst—half human, half the shivering, blurry grayness that was their outlines. But he saw the hideous smiles stretch over their faces when they saw Dandio was alone.

Not entirely alone though—Rygal felt a sudden determination rise inside him. He stumbled back towards the horse, where Dandio's second sword hung from the saddlebag. He drew it free, a little surprised at the weight, but felt its balance in his grip at the same time.

The three Hazes were stepping closer. Dandio stood unmoving, his sword held ready, his green eyes rapidly analyzing the situation.

Then he lunged—so fast Rygal hardly realized he'd moved. His sword slashed across the chest of the nearest Haze as he pivoted and cut at a second monster.

The Haze that had been wounded hardly reacted. It simply looked down at the huge wound in its chest, then watched as the flesh seemed to knit itself back together. Then it stepped forward with deadly speed. It kicked Dandio in the chest as the Liznee lunged forward, sending him crashing back into the bracken.

"Hey!" Rygal shouted, stepping forward, raising the short sword. His voice was small and weak in the sudden silence. All three Hazes turned their heads slowly, their shifting eyes fixing on him.

A new kind of fear suddenly filled him, and he realized, in an instant, that this had been a bad decision.

Dandio took advantage of the brief distraction, leaping to his feet and lunging forward. He raised his hands, red light glowing in his palms, and a blast of crackling red lightning shot from his hands. The blast hit the closest Haze and sent it reeling sideways, knocking it to its knees.

The other two Hazes both raised their weapons, the larger charging towards Dandio. Dandio parried its sword and ducked under another blow, then fired another blast of crackling red. But the smaller Haze stepped forward, flung its blade aside, and raised its own hands. Fire shot from its palms. The two blasts met in midair with a blinding crackling flash.

Rygal stumbled back, shielding his eyes from the light—when his vision cleared, he saw the third Haze towering over him. He shouted again and swung the sword. The blade felt unfamiliar and much heavier than he had expected in his hands. The two blades met—the Haze raised its sword over him again, swinging a brutal second blow—Rygal managed to drop back, but couldn't get his blade up and out of the way in time, and the blades met with a ringing crash that wrenched the sword from his hands.

Rygal fell back, heart pounding. The Haze towered over him, its lifeless eyes filled with hate. Rygal jumped to his feet and ran back, stooping to pick up his sword. But the Haze moved just as fast, slashing at his neck—as he stooped, the blade missed, and slashed instead across his shoulder and upper arm.

Rygal only felt the impact at first, as if he'd been hit with a tree limb—and then the pain began, penetrating, searing hot pain in his arm. The blade had cut deep down his arm, and he could feel warm blood pooling in his palm.

Dazed at the pain and the sight of his own blood, he fell back, swaying, feeling himself falling. The Haze had stepped back… it wasn't trying to finish him off, nor was it leaving him, it seemed to be waiting for something…

His vision seemed to be blurring, and he took another step back, blinking rapidly. Through the growing numbness in his chest, something else filled him, a sense of power, hate, greed, and the overwhelming desire—not desire, it was a need—to kill any living thing in sight. *Kill, kill, kill,* a dull, whispering voice was speaking inside his head, a voice he didn't recognize—

Then a blast of red lightning sent the Haze stumbling back. Dandio caught Rygal as he swayed and hauled him up on the black horse, then sprang up behind. With a snap of the reins, they left the Hazes behind.

Rygal coughed. The repetitive jarring of the horse sent pain back into his arm. What just happened? His brain couldn't comprehend what had happened back there, where those dark thoughts had come from.

The numbness was setting in again, much stronger than before…if they could only have killed those monsters right then, then perhaps—

Dizziness engulfed him for a moment, and he nearly fell from the saddle, suddenly feeling sick. He felt Dandio grip him tightly, holding him in place.

"I told you to run," the Liznee reprimanded him softly. "Even both of us could not have stopped the Hazes." He paused. "How do you feel? Is it just your arm?"

"I'm…" Rygal didn't want to look like a wimp in front of Dandio Ki, but the numbness and that chilling voice back in the glade scared him somehow. "I can't feel my arm. And I'm cold."

He was very cold—now that he thought about it, he was much too cold considering he had just been fighting and running.

Dandio's grip tightened slightly. "All right—all right. Don't think about it now. Right now I want you to focus—picture everything you knew in Gayrile, all the people, what you did, anything. Talk to me about that."

That was an odd order, Rygal thought, but he did, and in a moment he was rambling on about life in Gayrile. He talked about the soldiers in the market, about getting bread from Mr. Kellis, about going fishing with Norrin, about swimming in the bay when the weather was warm enough—

The numbness faded slightly as he talked, and the searing pain returned. He tried not to think about it.

The horse slowed to a trot, then stopped, and Dandio lifted him from the saddle. They were on the ground now, walking swiftly. He could hear snatches of sound, glimpses of his comrades and what they were doing, woven in through the gray fog that was slowly filling his head. The dull voice was speaking again, whispering in his head—*give in, let it take you, become one of us…*

"Rygal? Rygal—is he hurt? What happened? What did they do?" That was Dusty, her voice filled with fear…

*Give in…*

"He stayed an' fought, then? Is 'e all right?" Glentree's voice, with the same note of worry. Rygal felt himself being lowered to the ground, to a mat by the fire…

*Let it take you… you will be powerful, great, mighty…*

Dandio's voice cut in, talking quickly—to Glentree occasionally, but mostly to Rygal. Rygal wished he would go away—he felt so tired, and now Dandio was doing something to his arm—white hot pain seared up into his shoulder, deafening the voice for a moment, and he cried out.

"Easy," Dandio told him softly. "Keep talking."

Rygal realized that he had been talking the whole time, murmuring senseless things about Gayrile—about how they had to wash the windows in the summer because in the winter the soap was bad for the glass, about how Norrin didn't like his toast cut down the middle, about how Rygal's bedroom walls were painted gray, and he had always wanted to paint them blue—

The voice was fading away, sounding more desperate—*fool, what are you doing? Don't you want to be powerful? He's ruining you, can't you feel it—give in, let the spell take you—*

"Hold on, Rygal," Dandio said quietly, and Rygal took a breath before he kept talking. *"My father is named Maran, and he died because of Safacon—that's why I couldn't join the soldiers in the market, does that make sense?"*

"It does," Dandio said gently. "Sleep—try to sleep."

Rygal saw the Liznee's blurry outline move as Dandio stood, talking briefly to Glentree.

"He was struck by one of their swords—I don't know how better to treat that kind of wound. It's in him now—only time will tell."

"He's a strong 'un. He might make it."

Glentree's voice… that was the last thing Rygal heard.

. . . . . .

Until he suddenly awoke.

Rygal blinked, his eyes reluctantly adjusting to the midday light. *Where am I?* He wasn't on Gayrile… where was Norrin…?

Then, slowly, everything came back to him. Being washed here in the storm. Meeting Dusty and Tag. Joining Dandio Ki and Glentree. The three Hazes, and their shapeless, lifeless faces—

He tried to sit up, then regretted it as pain shot through his shoulder, and he settled back again. Dusty, who was sitting across the fire, looked up. Her face was so tired and filled with worry that it made her look much older. But her eyes lit up as she saw him. "You're awake! I was pretty sure you'd make it, but I wasn't sure—you were all still and gray—it was awful." She stopped, looking at him for a long moment. "You're all right? I mean—you know where we are?"

"I think so," Rygal said slowly. "How long have I been asleep?"

"A little over a day," Dusty said, and grinned as Rygal looked at her in shock. "You needed it. Especially after that wound."

"Yeah…" Rygal murmured. The memories were coming back in fragments now, almost like trying to remember a bad dream. He remembered the pain, and the strange cold numbness—he remembered rambling on about Gayrile, which had been odd, especially because whenever he had been doing that, his arm hurt worse…

And he remembered that horrible cold voice, hissing and spitting in his head…

"What exactly happened?" he asked finally. "What… what did that blade do to me?"

Dusty hesitated. "I… Dandio didn't want to tell you. You probably don't need to worry about it now though. You're fine now. What could have happened isn't important."

"What could have happened?" Rygal prompted.

Dusty hesitated again for a long moment. "The Hazes… their blades are… enchanted, or something, and if you get stabbed, then you… turn into one of them."

Rygal stared at her in shock. Dusty looked down, uncomfortable. Rygal could hardly find the words. "But—how—I might have—" He remembered that sudden numbness, the dark thoughts that had crossed his mind right after the blow, and the voice in his head…

Was that what the Hazes felt like? Cold, numb, knowing nothing but the bidding of their master as he hissed his instructions in their heads, controlling them…

Dusty seemed to guess what he was thinking. "Don't worry. You're all right now. You're here."

Rygal nodded, dismissing what could have happened for the present. He put on his shirt and glanced around. They were in another glade, this one a little bigger than the last one, surrounded by towering birch trees. He glanced at where the horses were tied, and was startled to see two more.

"Whose are those?" he asked, nodding to the horses.

Dusty nodded to the other side of the glade, where Dandio and Glentree sat and talked. A third figure sat with them, speaking earnestly with Dandio.

"He got here about an hour ago. He's one of Dandio's lieutenants in the army."

Rygal moved toward them, stretching out his shoulder gently. While it was very stiff and felt bruised, that searing pain was gone.

The newcomer wore a simple gray outfit under a leather jerkin, light shoes, and a mottled green cloak. A quiver of arrows was strapped to his back, and he held a longbow across his knees. His hair was strawberry-blond, pulled back at the nape of his neck. The chiseled features, pointed ears, and keen eyes marked him as an Elf. He was talking to Dandio as Rygal and Dusty approached.

"… at any rate, we have tried that method, of water, but I don't think that's the key. There must be some other way to stop them. And once we stop them, I am sure we could help them."

"I'd bet you're right at that, but the issue is how to do that," Dandio murmured. He glanced up as Rygal and Dusty reached them, and smiled warmly. "Glad to see you're on your feet. How does your arm feel?"

"Stiff," Rygal admitted, and glanced at the Elf. His eyes had a quick, calculating look in them that told Rygal he would be a dangerous opponent. But they were friendly as he smiled.

"Dandio tells me you faced the Hazes," he said to Rygal. "That was quite brave."

Rygal felt himself redden slightly at the praise. "Well… all I did was get stabbed, honestly. I didn't really do much."

The Elf smiled. "Honesty is a good trait for a warrior to have. So I applaud you."

Dandio smiled as well, then turned to Rygal. "Rygal, this is Llyrion son of Llio, one of my oldest comrades and friends. He will be with us for a little while, I hope."

"At least until I continue my journey west," Llyrion said.

Rygal sat down near Dandio, remembering his question. "Dandio, those Hazes… do you think they'll follow us?"

"They might," Dandio said grimly. "At any rate we can do very little about them until we are back in Sia, at which point we can hopefully develop some sort of strategy against them."

"They cannot be completely without weakness," Llyrion mused.

"There must be some way to stop them, some flaw in Kado's spell. And once we figure that out…"

"No more Hazes," Dandio finished for him.

"How will we figure that out?" Dusty asked, cocking her head slightly to the side.

"The only way we figure anything out. We watch. We observe. We gather facts, use trial and error, until we've got it," Dandio told her.

That sounded like something Norrin would say, Rygal thought, and found his interest increase. "Then… you think they could be changed back, to their original forms?"

Llyrion spoke. "We believe they might. And that is the purpose of my quest."

# 6

## The Fate of the Hazes

*Could the Hazes be changed back?* Rygal looked at Llyrion curiously.

Dusty looked puzzled. "But… how?" she asked finally.

"Well, that is what I plan to find out, with help from Commander Dandio," the Elf replied, looking to the Liznee.

Dandio nodded. "So far, all we know of the Hazes is that they are a seemingly indestructible force created by Kado. However, Kado couldn't create them from nothing—he has apparently either bribed or tricked many men into serving him. Then, he turns them into Hazes with his spell."

"Like what he tried to do to me," Rygal said slowly, with a shiver of fear. He didn't like thinking about those last moments of consciousness, thinking of Kado's hissing voice in his brain.

Dandio nodded again. "Safacon himself is a great sorcerer—no doubt Kado fancies himself equal."

"Which may be why he's this far south at all," Llyrion pointed out. "Kado is no fool, and neither is Safacon. But even if Kado is cunning, he's also ambitious. My guess is that the moment the Hazes were created and operational, Safacon sent him south to see what they could do. A test mission for his new creations."

There was a pause. Dusty, sitting beside Glentree, looked up at Dandio. "Then how do you think we can turn them back?"

Dandio's brow was furrowed slightly in thought. Finally he looked up. "To be honest with all of you, I didn't think such a thing was possible. I was sure that once the Hazes were Hazes, there could be no reversing of the spell, and our focus should be on their destruction, not salvation. Up till a few hours ago."

"What happened then?" Rygal asked.

Dandio looked right at him, and suddenly he understood. "You were injured, Rygal. The spell had begun. But you're here now. I know for a fact that it was nothing my medical services could have done, but somehow the spell was stopped."

"You told me to talk," Rygal said, thinking. "You told me to think about Gayrile."

"And so your focus was on your present life," Llyrion mused, glancing at Dandio. "That's something the Hazes don't have. Their minds are completely washed of their past lives."

"What if we could help them remember?" Dusty asked. "Help them remember everything they had before Kado?"

"If we could, that'd be quite an accomplishment," Glentree agreed. "But I fear that'd be a wee bit difficult. Besides that, it can't be as easy as just talkin' to them."

"True," Dandio agreed. "It worked for Rygal, but only, I think, because he was still in the first stages of the process."

Llyrion looked at Dandio again, his face thoughtful. "There might be a link there, Dandio. We couldn't just talk to them, obviously, because they would only become agitated and probably aggressive. But if something could be done to help them… it'd be something like that."

"I agree with you there." Dandio looked thoughtful. He shook his head. "Well, the Hazes will have to wait for the present. At the moment I think it'd be best to discuss what is to be done now." He looked at Llyrion. "You plan to ride to Elimar?"

Llyrion nodded. "My father has influence there—he can help rally the Elves to the Liznee's cause against Kado. And I hope to learn more of the Hazes on the way."

"Iriam would know," Dandio murmured.

Glentree glanced at him. "No one's heard word from 'im in years. Not since the war. Ya think he'd help?"

"If we could still contact him, I'm sure he would," Dandio said calmly. "But the problem is getting word to him, as after the fall of the last queen, I think he returned to the area around the Forest of Light."

"Mmm," Glentree murmured. He stood. "Well then, what about the young'uns?" He nodded to Rygal and Dusty, and Tag, who was asleep by the fire.

"I want to help," Rygal said immediately. "If there's a way to stop Kado and turn the Hazes back, then I want in."

"Me too," Dusty said promptly.

The three adults exchanged a glance. "I cannot risk leading you into a potential war zone," Dandio said uncertainly. "Glentree and I will escort you north to Caer Sia, and then resume our mission to the southern villages."

"We'd lose a lot of time," Glentree pointed out doubtfully. "Two days travel north, maybe longer if we have to detour around the mountains… and then at least a three-day trip to Tinkeeyo…"

"True," Dandio said, shaking his head, "but it can't be helped."

Llyrion looked at Dandio, suddenly thoughtful. "What if they came with me?" he said. "I ride southwest, to Elimar, away from where we expect the Hazes are. If we encountered anything I doubt it would be Kado."

Rygal looked up hopefully. Elimar was an Elven town, a good day's ride from here, just within the Coonsian border. While smaller than Caer Sia, it would be the largest city he had ever been to.

Dandio still looked uneasy. "Hazes or no, the path to Elimar is no safe one."

"Neither is Caer Sia," Llyrion pointed out, arching an eyebrow. He looked at Rygal and Dusty. "I'll keep them safe. They can stay with my family when we reach Elimar, at least until it's safe for them to go north and home."

"We won't get in the way," Rygal said, looking hopefully at Dandio. "Dusty and I can both hunt and fish pretty well—we can help."

The shadow of a smile crossed Dandio's face, though he still looked unsure. But at last he nodded. "Very well, then. Take them to Elimar, Llyrion. Let them stay with your family, and Glentree and I can pick them up and take them to Sia on our way back from the Southern Fiefs."

Rygal felt a shiver of both excitement and fear. He was going to Elimar, to Coonsia—that was a country of legends, of battle and fame—Kado was there, with the Hazes, farther north than the Elven towns, of course, but…

They probably wouldn't run into him… but still, the thought of facing the horrific Hazes again sent chills of foreboding down his spine.

"Well, then! That's settled," Llyrion said, standing and clapping his hands. "We ride this evening."

"Very well," Dandio said, finally smiling. He stood. "We had best pack up camp."

They got to work quickly. Rygal helped Llyrion make ready. The tall, quick-thinking Elven warrior gave him instructions as they talked.

"We'll have to make room for two riders on the pack horse," Llyrion told him as they crossed to the two horses. "I won't want you both to have to walk the whole way."

"How far is it to Elimar?" Rygal asked him curiously as they moved the packs from the back of the horse.

Llyrion thought a moment. "Not too far. Two good days of travel will get us there."

"And… what if there are Hazes?"

"I doubt there will be. Although…" he paused, studying Rygal carefully. Then he shook his head briskly. "Well—if we run into them, we can outrun them, at least, just as you and Dandio did yesterday."

Rygal repacked one of the bags and attempted to lift it back to its place behind the saddle—it was heavier than he'd thought, and the movement sent a jolt of pain into his shoulder. He lowered it again.

"Need help?" Llyrion asked kindly. He stepped over and swung the bag up, then strapped it down behind the saddle.

"Thanks," Rygal panted, testing his arm carefully. It still ached, which wasn't surprising, but nothing like the searing pain from before.

"How does it feel?" Llyrion asked.

"Sore," Rygal admitted with a grin. "But not like when I got slashed. More like I have the worst bruise I've ever had."

"That sounds about right," Llyrion said, shaking his head. "Well, that's quite a wound to end your first battle with. Definitely something you could brag about at home."

"Yeah," Rygal said, grinning. This reminded him of something. "You said earlier that you think the Hazes could be changed back—that we might defeat them that way."

Llyrion nodded, and Rygal continued. "I thought Kado's spell was permanent—when Dandio told us about them last night, it didn't sound like there was even a possibility of undoing the spell…"

"Well, I won't give up the notion yet," Llyrion said. There was something in his tone that caught Rygal's attention, some emotion there… hope, determination, sorrow…

Dusty reappeared, carrying several flasks of water. "Here we go. Dandio says we should refill again at the first spring we see—he says the streams along the border aren't drinkable."

"Well, we'll do that before we reach the border," Llyrion reassured her. He glanced up, studying her for a moment. "By the way— what Clan are you?"

Dusty looked surprised and rather pleased. "Mara-N'Tell. How do you know about the Clans?"

"My brother was a merchant—he had stories of his dealings with the Wildkids, before the time of Kircadash when our contact with them was severed." Llyrion looked interested. "The N'Tell—that's on the eastern side of Kasabren, isn't it?"

"No, we moved to the western coast a few years ago, after the Jenna attacks."

"Jenna?" Rygal said, feeling a bit left out.

"Warriors in the east, in Sikhazi," Dusty informed him. "They're like orcs, sort of, but more human, and they—"

"I know what they are," Rygal said impatiently. "I didn't know they attacked outside of their country."

"It's become more frequent in the past few years," Llyrion said grimly. He fastened the straps on the final saddle bag. "Right, then—we're all packed up, I think it's nearly time to go."

Dandio met them on the road astride his horse on the cross road heading south. He clasped Llyrion's hand. "Be safe. Be swift. Stay away from the Hazes."

"Yes, sir," Llyrion said with a nod.

"And send word once you reach Elimar," Dandio added as he and Glentree started south. "We'll see you there in a few weeks."

"Travel safe," Llyrion called, then clipped his heels to his horse's sides. Rygal and Dusty, mounted on the packhorse, urged the animal forward, and they started down the trail.

Tag trotted after them, his tail wagging. "Hurry up, Tag," Dusty called with a grin. "We're going to Coonsia."

# 7

## The Road West

They rode west for the remainder of the day, moving their way through the dense woods. Rygal had never seen forests like these. On Gayrile, most of the trees were stunted and shabby after growing so close to the sea. Out here, the trees grew taller than the tallest building he'd ever seen, some wider around than he would have been able to reach around if he'd tried.

It was getting increasingly difficult to see which direction they were headed—the forest formed an impenetrable labyrinth around them. Llyrion rode confidently ahead—the Elf looked right at home.

"Are we getting close to Coonsia?" Rygal called to him finally. Behind him, Dusty was nodding off. Night was falling.

Llyrion reined in, glanced at them, and then smiled. "We're nearing the border. Another few hours of riding will do it. But I think it can wait till morning."

Rygal's heart lifted, and he nudged Dusty. "Wake up. We're setting up camp."

"I'm not asleep," Dusty mumbled, sliding off the horse and moving to check on Tag. The young wolfhound looked worn out, but he wagged his tail as Dusty stroked his fur.

"Unload the packs," Llyrion instructed. "You can leave a few of them tied on—it'll save us time tomorrow when we pack up again. Just loosen the straps to give the horses a break."

Rygal did as instructed and removed the pack that contained food and water. Llyrion handed him and Dusty their bedrolls, which they spread out on the ground.

"How's your arm?" Llyrion asked as he collected tinder for a fire.

Rygal stretched his shoulder experimentally. "Better. It's not as sore now."

"Well, it will be," Llyrion said with a wry smile. "Let me know how it is in the morning—there's a numbing balm in the packs that will help ease some of the pain."

Rygal nodded, hesitating a moment. He wasn't sure he wanted the next question answered, but he felt like he had to know. "Llyrion… how was Dandio able to… stop me from turning into a Haze?"

A brief pause. Dusty looked up, glancing from Rygal to Llyrion, with the same uncertain curiosity as Rygal felt.

Llyrion seemed to be thinking through his reply. "Well… I'll admit I'm not entirely sure. I've seen what the Haze's spell can do, Rygal, and I think you may be one of the first—if not the only— person to survive its effects."

"Really?" This startled him. He knew it was a surprising thing that he had survived, but he didn't know it was that rare for someone to do so.

Llyrion nodded slowly, looking thoughtful. "In answer to your question, I know part of it was that Dandio was able to get you warm quickly, which was important. And he kept your mind from slipping away—did he tell you to start talking about a specific thing?"

"Yeah," Rygal said slowly, remembering. It hadn't made sense then, but now he understood.

Dusty glanced between the two of them, still looking confused. "But Llyrion—if Rygal's the only person who survived the Hazes' effects, then how'd Dandio know about that? How did he know how to help?"

"Dandio and Glentree, as well as myself, have been studying the Hazes and Kado for quite some time," Llyrion told her. "It wasn't guaranteed to work. And I know that another aspect of it was that Rygal's wound, though painful, was not severe. A larger wound would have ensured another warrior in Kado's army."

Rygal swallowed hard, suddenly chilled by the aspect of how close he'd come. "So… what about the other Hazes?"

"The other Hazes are not like you were. You were on the brink. They've already jumped. Their minds are fully polluted by Kado's spell, and it will take more than a fire's warmth and a discussion of their past to free them." Llyrion set a few more limbs on the fire, then settled down, leaning back against a tree. "However impossible it seems, though, know that I am determined to find the solution."

The same emotion Rygal had noticed earlier crossed the Elf's face as he said that—sadness, grief, mingled with determination. He wondered what it meant. But he decided not to bring it up.

Llyrion straightened. "No more questions about the Hazes for now. Let's talk of other things."

"Well, I was wondering something," Dusty said, her brow wrinkled slightly. "It's about Dandio. Back in the glade, when the Hazes came—he shot fire from his hands at them."

"It wasn't fire—it looked like red lightning," Rygal told her. He looked at Llyrion. "He did it in the battle against the Hazes—it was the only thing that pushed them back."

"Well, that's not sorcery or anything like that," Llyrion told them with a slight smile. "That is the natural power—the natural Essence of a Liznee. It is as essential to them as the blood in their veins, and with skill, they can master its power and wield it in battle."

Rygal was startled. "You mean—that's normal? They can just… do that?"

"Normal for the Liznees, and for several other species on Orlell," Llyrion said. He thought a moment, trying to decide how to explain it. "Every living thing in Orlell has an Essence given by the High Light, Rygal—the very life inside you. That Essence manifests itself differently depending on your species. There are three categories— the Cantrians, the Fyrocrians, and the Netrocrians. Cantrians are the most common—their Essence cannot be fired, and remains inside of us. Beings like humans and Elves."

He paused, then continued. "The Fyrocrians are light wielders—the Star people, Liznees, even some dragons. Their power may show itself as fire or lightning. For the Liznees, as you saw earlier, they are filled with power that manifests as red, lightning-like flames. Unlike other beings, Liznees only have so much Essence that they can fire at once—it's vital to them."

"You mean…they could die if they use too much," Rygal realized.

"Yes, although it rarely happens," Llyrion said. He leaned back against the tree, staring up at the stars.

Dusty spoke, her voice soft. "And…the Netrocrians?" she asked, searching for the word. "Are they like Hazes?"

Llyrion shook his head. "The Hazes are artificial beings. And unless the original being was a Fyrocrian or the like, then the Hazes have no power to fire." Rygal remembered the smaller Haze, which had countered Dandio's blast with fire, and understood what he meant. Llyrion hesitated. "The Netrocrians are…something else entirely."

He hesitated again, but they both wanted an answer, and so he continued. "When the High Light made all things, He intended the Netrocrians to be keepers of peace, with great power. But they rebelled against Him and disappeared, exiled, becoming creatures of ice and darkness. There are very few known Netrocrians in Orlell—most of them have been stopped by the Liznees long ago. Fire is deadly to them, and they fear it, which is how many of them were stopped before. There are a few still, some allies, even. But we know very little of them."

The atmosphere had grown chill again. Llyrion finally straightened abruptly. "All this talk about Hazes and Netrocrians, and neither of you will sleep a wink. Get to sleep, both of you. I'll take the first watch."

Rygal settled down on his mat, his thoughts full of other beings, other species, until he finally drifted off. The hissing voice of Kado echoed weakly in his half-conscious mind, clawing at his thoughts, still relentlessly pursuing his waking mind.

# 8

∽ ∽ ∽ ∽ ∽ ∽ ∽ ∽ ∽

## *The Watcher in the Shadows*

Morning dawned gray and cloudy. Early winter frost covered the ground, and Rygal woke shivering. The fire, though still smoldering, had burned down, and sometime in the night he'd rolled away from it. He scooted closer to the embers.

"It appears we may have to detour," Llyrion told them over breakfast.

Rygal looked at him, startled. "What? Why?"

Llyrion pointed west. "The border is about a six-hour ride that direction, as I said last night. I scouted that way a little earlier this morning. No Hazes, thankfully, but the trail leading there practically reeks of Orc. No doubt they've joined with Kado too."

"Orcs?" Dusty repeated, sounding surprised. "I thought they were neutral."

"They're mercenaries, most of them. They'll stay neutral until someone offers them enough pay to fight." Llyrion looked frustrated. "We're going to have to go north, around them, and take another road past the border and to Elimar."

"But aren't the Hazes in the north?" Rygal asked worriedly.

"I doubt it—by this point the Hazes have either pursued Dandio

92

and Glentree south or rejoined Kado near Caer Sia. I don't expect them to be lingering around," Llyrion said. He shook his head. "Well, either way we can't stay here for long. Finish eating, then let's pack up and get going."

It was frustrating to head in a different direction than they needed to go, but Rygal knew they had to avoid the orcs along the road. Llyrion was a skilled warrior, but he wouldn't be able to take on an entire army of orcs alone.

They left the western road and took a new path, this one curving gradually north. The horses plodded along purposefully, their hooves crunching on the frosty gravel.

"Do you s'pose Dandio and Glentree made it south?" Dusty asked presently, her eyes scanning the wooded terrain.

"Probably," Rygal guessed. "I don't know how far the Southern Fiefs are from here, though, so I don't know how long it'd take them."

He knew the Southern Fiefs were in the southeasternmost corner of Coonsia, but since he wasn't entirely sure where they were, he had no idea of guessing how far Dandio and Glentree would have to travel. He hoped they'd get there safely. Although, he realized the danger would probably lie in coming back, when they had to pass through the area with the Hazes…

He shook the thoughts away.

They stopped for a brief rest around noon. Llyrion passed around bread and water. "We've made good time," he announced, looking satisfied. "I believe we can take the next road west, and resume our original course."

"What about the orcs?" Rygal asked.

"I've seen no sign of them coming this way," Llyrion said.

"Maybe the ones back there were just traveling through," Dusty suggested. "Maybe they weren't with Kado at all."

"Maybe," Llyrion mused, "but I'm not sure. We'll have to see."

They mounted back up and continued riding. While the detour had been brief, it had still cost them time, and by evening, they were still only a little closer to the border.

"All that for maybe nothing at all," Rygal couldn't help grumbling.

Llyrion heard him, and smiled slightly. "Better safe than sorry. At any rate there's no harm done. We'll camp here again and move toward the border tomorrow."

They settled down for the night. Rygal was tired, but he quickly volunteered for first watch. "You stayed up all of last night," he told Llyrion. "Dusty and I can take watch tonight."

"Well, all right," Llyrion relented, smiling his thanks. He lay down beside the fire and was soon asleep.

Rygal sat on a log, his back to the fire, staring out into the shadowed wood. The strange creaks and groans of the tree branches and the rustling of small animals moving through the bracken didn't startle him like they had when he'd first come here. He thought for a moment, realizing in surprise that it had only been four days since he had been swept here. It felt like longer.

He wondered how Norrin fared, if he had searched for him, if he had given up. No, Norrin wouldn't give up, Rygal was sure of it. But eventually he would realize that Rygal was no longer gripped by the current… or would he? What if Norrin just kept sailing, searching for him? Rygal wished there was some way to get word to him.

"I'm here, Norrin," he whispered, staring into the darkness.

His mind strayed back to his last conversation with Norrin, about the sorcerer Safacon—about him trying to take over Gayrile, and about the Guardians forced into hiding. Yet Norrin had withheld quite a bit of information from him about Safacon—Rygal was sure of that. But why? What could be so secret that even he couldn't know?

He wasn't sure, and his tired mind could only focus on one thing right now—and that was keeping awake while on watch. After two hours, he got up and roused Dusty, who took over for him. He settled down by the fire and was soon asleep, thoughts of Gayrile filling his mind.

. . . . . .

Two people were talking in his head, one sounding far away, the other surprisingly close, hissing in his brain—

*Wake. Wake. Embrace the spell and become the monster you fear.*

He stirred, unable to sort the voice out from waking or sleeping—there was a distant sound, he thought he heard Llyrion's voice, then Dusty's, quite close.

"Rygal! Wake up!"

*Join us… you will be great, powerful—*

Rygal jolted awake, pain flaring in his shoulder as he did so. Kado's hissing voice vanished. Tag was barking. Dusty crouched above him, shaking him. The look on her face confirmed the worst.

"What's wrong? Is it the—"

Something crashed through the trees off to his right—he turned his head, his blood chilling as he saw the shadowy, blurred shapes.

"Hazes!" Dusty screamed.

Rygal sprang upright, pulling Dusty behind him. Fear was pumping through him. There were three Hazes, all wielding weapons. They moved with a frightening speed, and their half-visible forms made them seem to vanish and reappear at different places.

"Get the horses!" came Llyrion's voice—the Elf was crouched in the bracken, an arrow nocked to his bowstring, eyes scanning the woods.

Rygal stumbled towards the horses, who were whinnying in fear and stamping the ground. Tag was growling, hackles up, but had huddled back by the horses.

The hissing voice of Kado and the dull ache in his shoulder made Rygal sway for an instant, fear gripping him as he faced the Hazes again. Then reason returned, and he turned to Dusty. "Let's go, hurry—as soon as we're mounted we'll get Llyrion."

Dusty nodded and moved to the fire, grabbing the pack containing the food and water, and the second pack, which contained the maps. Rygal pulled a flaming branch from the fire and moved toward the Hazes, brandishing it.

"Get back!" he shouted, moving to Llyrion's side.

The Hazes hesitated at the sight of fire, but they seemed to realize at the same time that Dandio was not here. They moved forward again. Llyrion fired an arrow into the closest warrior's face, making it stagger back. The second Haze went at Rygal, who swung the burning branch straight through its ghostly form. The warrior stumbled, the swirling oblivion of its torso blurring for an instant, but then the wound faded and it straightened.

Rygal threw the branch at it, then ran towards Dusty as Llyrion drew the Hazes' attention back. The Elf fired a second arrow, which buried itself in the Haze's chest.

Rygal moved to Dusty, who was climbing into the saddle. "Get up," he murmured, his legs actually shaking with fear, "hurry…"

Llyrion fired a third shot into the Haze's forearm, which made it drop its sword. Rygal handed Dusty the reins. "I'm going to help him—if we both go down, ride as fast as you can north."

Dusty looked at him in disbelief, then fear. "No… I won't just—"

One of the Hazes wrenched a bough from the nearest tree, then flung it at the Elf. It hit Llyrion, hard, across the shoulder blades, sending him sprawling, his bow falling from his grasp. The Hazes, sure of their victory now, moved forward.

"Llyrion!" Rygal cried in alarm, running forward before he knew what he was doing. He saw, out of the corner of his eye, as Dusty sprang from the saddle and ran after him. Rygal lifted the Haze's dropped sword, swinging it at them, making them turn away from Llyrion and advance on him. A stone struck the Haze in the face—Dusty stooped beside the fire, holding another stone at the ready.

"Back!" Rygal shouted at them. But this time, the Hazes barely responded to his voice. The nearest warrior gripped the blade of the sword in both hands and wrenched it from Rygal's grasp. Its face was frozen in a triumphant grin as it moved forward.

They were trapped—Llyrion was semiconscious on the far side of the glade, Rygal saw him trying to reach his bow—he could feel nothing beyond cold, paralyzing fear. Dusty screamed in terror as the Haze reached for her.

And that was when a ray of dark blue ice struck the lead Haze in the chest, making it stagger back. Rygal looked up in shock. The other two Hazes had seen something too; they were falling back, retreating—

Another blast of ice struck the closest Haze again, and it fell back as the blows began, striking it repeatedly in the chest. Ice coiled around the Haze's body, gripping it, freezing it—the Haze writhed, making horrible, inhuman groans, for the first time feeling true pain.

Then the ice stopped. Before Rygal and Dusty, still gripping the sword, was the frozen corpse of the Haze.

For an instant there was total silence. The other two Hazes had fled. Rygal finally turned towards the tree line where the ice had come from, and felt his heartbeat quicken.

The shadowy outline of a tall, hooded figure stood there. Rygal saw it lower its hands calmly, and then it strode forward. As the early light of dawn fell on the newcomer, Rygal saw the dark gray skin, the red eyes, and the lowered hands still glittering softly with ice.

*A Netrocrian.*

"Troubles with the Hazes, child?" the Netrocrian asked softly, his voice as cold and clear as the ice he had just used.

Rygal stood in his place, fear still coursing through him. A Netrocrian… he was certain, the ice and the darkness about the newcomer left no doubt. A creature that had remained in exile for centuries, now standing before them.

"I—I don't—we didn't—" he stammered, totally at a loss, not sure what to say. Dusty only stared, her mouth slightly open, her eyes wide.

The stranger removed his hood. He had no hair on his head or face, like Dandio, and his chiseled features held a wisdom—even kindness—that surprised Rygal. "I am not about to hurt you, boy," he said quietly, his voice as deep and soft as the thrum of a bowstring. "If you are an enemy of the Hazes, then I am on your side."

"You're a Netrocrian," Dusty said slowly before Rygal could stop her.

The red eyes twinkled slightly. "I am. But as I said before, I am on your side. My name is Iriam."

# 9

꩜ ꩜ ꩜ ꩜ ꩜ ꩜ ꩜ ꩜ ꩜

# In the Company of an Ice-Wielder

*Iriam.* The name was vaguely familiar, but Rygal couldn't place it. The tall, dark figure before him was still imposing, but some of his fear had faded.

"Now, who are you?" Iriam asked, moving forward. "And why have you fallen on the wrong side of the Hazes?"

"I—my name's Rygal. Rygal of Gayrile," he said, trying to sound older than he was. "My companions and I are traveling to Elimar," he added vaguely. He didn't fully trust this Netrocrian, no matter if he had just saved their lives.

Iriam arched an eyebrow. "So I assumed. That does not answer why you are being pursued by Hazes if you are mere travelers, however." He scrutinized them carefully, those penetrating crimson eyes piercing into Rygal's blue.

On the other side of the clearing, Llyrion had got to his feet painfully, and approached slowly, one hand on his bow. Iriam's eyes flicked over to him, and suddenly his face changed from suspicious to friendly concern. "Lieutenant Llyrion Tarash. I assume Dandio sent you? Is he nearby?"

Rygal looked at the stranger in surprise. Llyrion still seemed

100

dazed, but he shook his head slowly. "No—he is not here, unfortunately. He sent us to Elimar, but he mentioned we might be able to find you."

"Where is he headed, then?"

"The Southern Fiefs." Llyrion sank to the ground again, looking exhausted. A streak of blood creased his face.

Iriam nodded. "Come. We will talk somewhere safe." He turned and moved back into the forest.

Rygal looked at Llyrion, totally at a loss, but slowly realizing they were no longer in immediate danger.

"It's all right," Llyrion told them, as Rygal helped him to his feet. "We can trust him. He's one of the king's most trusted advisors."

"He's a Netrocrian," Dusty said softly, looking unsure. Tag nosed her hand; he was still trembling from the encounter with the Hazes.

Llyrion nodded in response to her statement. "He is. And he's loyal to the king and to the High Light. He's not one of the rebels I told you about last night."

They moved through the trees, following the tall shadow before them. Rygal noted the striking differences between Iriam and Dandio as they did. Well, not physical differences—they actually looked a little similar there, except Iriam's face was older, wiser. And while Dandio seemed to radiate energy and fiery determination, Iriam was calm and cool, as complex as a Fyrocrian but in a different way somehow.

Rygal couldn't quite place it, but he could somehow sense that, despite Iriam's foreboding appearance, he was someone to trust.

And he was clearly a valuable ally.

They walked for maybe twenty minutes, until they reached the opening of a cave. Iriam stooped slightly to enter, and motioned for the others to follow. Rygal hesitated warily.

"Go on," Llyrion said at last. Rygal nodded and entered. Dusty followed, after tethering the horses outside. It was very dark almost instantly. Rygal blinked but could still see nothing. He heard Iriam call him from the left, turned a corner, and—

Stepped into what appeared to be an ordinary parlor. He blinked in surprise. To his left, a fire blazed merrily on the hearth, and three circular windows along the ceiling let in the sunlight. Rygal could see grass growing level to the windows, and knew they were below ground.

The room was furnished with two armchairs near the fire, and a table covered in worn yellow papers and scrolls. Ancient books filled the shelves. A large globe was set beside the table, and as Rygal approached, he was surprised to see the names of cities and continents that he knew there. Coonsia, Daffodalion, Caer Sia, Fauna…even little Gayrile perched at the top of the globe.

"Is Orlell round?" he asked in surprise, forgetting their situation for a moment.

"So the Stars report," Iriam said with a faint smile as he stoked the fire.

"Then why don't we all walk around upside-down?" Dusty challenged.

Iriam arched an eyebrow. "Well, I suppose you should save that question for the High Light someday."

Dusty looked a little puzzled but remained quiet.

Llyrion collapsed weakly into an armchair, and Iriam had turned to examine the wound on his brow. "Not too deep—a decent concussion, but you will recover," he said at last, and fastened on a bandage. "Rest will help the ache. I will wake you if you are needed."

Llyrion nodded wearily, and in a few moments he had collapsed, the strain of the last few days and from his injury finally wearing him out.

Dusty went outside to check on Tag and tend to the horses, which left Rygal alone in the room with Iriam. He watched the dark stranger as subtly as he could manage as Iriam added another log to the fire, then moved to the window, then turned, quite suddenly.

"May I answer your question, or are you content to observe?" he asked.

Rygal flushed, feeling bad, then shrugged slightly. "I—I'm sorry—I just thought, well—I thought all the Netrocrians were… bad."

He saw a trace of sorrow cross Iriam's face. "Unfortunately you are not entirely wrong. At the beginning of Time, as I think you know, there was a great battle waged between those loyal to the High Light and His good world, and rebel Netrocrians who would see it twisted under them. Many Netrocrians turned away in their evil and pride. A few remained loyal, and that is what my people are. We became known as the Neutrals, neither Fyrocrian, nor supporting the Netrocrian rebels."

Rygal sat down, fascinated by the story. "Then—how do you know Dandio?"

Iriam smiled. "I was his father's advisor, long ago—longer ago than I care to remember. When Jan was crowned, I advised him too. He has grown to be a great king, strong and compassionate, and his brother just so." He nodded in approval. "In the years after the fall of the last human queen, Kircadash, I returned to these woods, and times have been relatively peaceful. Until now, it seems."

A shadow seemed to have fallen in the room. Dusty reappeared, returning to the globe model of Orlell and scrutinizing it carefully. Clearly fascinated by the concept, she began firing questions at Iriam, who answered patiently. He seemed to know a lot more about the world than Rygal had first assumed.

Rygal walked along the walls, studying the paintings and tapestries that hung on the walls. Many of them looked very old—the entire place had the feeling of wisdom and age, the smell of old books and forgotten memories.

It reminded him, suddenly, of Norrin, and he felt a pang of longing as he thought of the old fisherman.

He sensed someone was watching him, and turned to see Iriam studying him. "You have the eyes of one who has come far and seeks much," he said at last.

Rygal thought a moment. "I… I guess so," he said finally, "just not in the way I'd pictured. I know what I'm seeking, I think, just not how I'll find it." He shrugged slowly, not sure how to explain how he felt.

"Then what do you seek?" Iriam asked.

Rygal hesitated. "I want to help Gayrile. Ever since I was little, I wanted to do something. Stop Safacon and bring back peace and order to Gayrile. But… when I finally get the chance to do something, to fight—I'm not even there. I'm here. On the Mainland. Not like I pictured."

A faint smile touched the Neutral's face. "Sometimes, we can only control our actions, not our circumstances or our situation. That's up to the High Light to decide. All we can do is wait and see where His leading takes us."

Rygal nodded slowly. "I… I guess what I really want is to avenge my father. Rally the Guardians of Gayrile again, march on Safacon, make him pay for what he's done." It was odd, discussing these things with the Neutral, but not in a bad way.

"A noble cause if it has the right motives," Iriam reminded him. He paused. "You know, the purpose of the Guardians was never to create war," he added.

Rygal looked up in surprise. "Really?"

Iriam nodded. "Their mission was to keep the peace on Gayrile, to be guardians of the High Light's truths and to help the commonwealth understand them. I believe that may be the most glorious task of all—helping others."

"Then… they weren't… warriors?" Rygal said, a little disappointed.

Iriam smiled slightly. "Oh, they would fight without hesitation should a threat arise. But they never sought out war. I believe a true warrior seeks the glory in living each day given to him as well as he can, not glory at the expense of others."

"Like Kado," Dusty said from behind Rygal. She had been listening quietly.

"Like Kado," Iriam agreed. "His lust for power has cost many lives." He straightened. "Well—all this talk, and yet you have eaten nothing all morning. Let us eat, and we may talk more after."

# 10

## Grayline Swamp

Rygal woke just after sunrise. For a moment he lay in a fog of sleepy confusion, unsure of where he was. He lay in a small room, curled up in a pile of blankets. Then yesterday's events came back to him in a flash—running from the Hazes, Llyrion being injured, meeting the Neutral who had saved them—

He looked around, seeing that Llyrion and Dusty's beds were both empty. The faint sound—accompanied by a delicious smell—came drifting from the main room, the sound of sizzling bacon. His mouth watered at the prospect of a warm breakfast after all the cold meals on the trail. Last night's dinner had left him stuffed, but now he was hungry again.

He got up, stretching his stiff arm as he did so. The muscle around his shoulder felt tight and bruised, but some of the pain had faded. The closeness of the Hazes, he was beginning to realize, brought pain back into his wound.

Iriam was tending to the fire as Rygal entered the room. Over the fire was a pan that held the source of the smell—bacon, eggs, and potatoes.

"Good morning," Iriam said with a nod. "Sleep well, I hope?"

"Yep," Rygal said with a yawn, sitting down. He looked around. "Where's everyone else?"

"Dusty has taken her dog for a walk, and Llyrion is tending to the horses. He hopes to be on the trail today," Iriam told him.

"Good," Rygal said, staring into the fire. He watched as Iriam silently prepared the meal, a question forming in his mind. "Is it true that Netrocrians are afraid of fire? You don't seem to be."

Iriam glanced at him with a half-smile, and Rygal realized how rude that phrasing sounded. "I mean—sorry, I guess when Llyrion told us about them—it sounds like they can't be touched by fire."

"Well, you are partly right again," Iriam told him. "Most of us are as vulnerable to fire as you would be. Others are more so, darker ones. I have noted that it depends on the individual."

Rygal nodded quickly, not exactly understanding it, but somehow sensing the heaviness of the subject. "Where… are the others? The rebels? What happened to them?"

Iriam looked at him with the same half-smile. "Few of them are accounted for. They are not like Kado or the Hazes, you know. They are more cunning, more patient. They have remained in hiding for centuries, and even I do not know their whereabouts." His smile had faded.

The thought of creatures in hiding, with the same power as Iriam, biding their time to strike, sent chills down Rygal's back, and suddenly a shadow seemed to have been cast in the room.

Iriam seemed to guess his thoughts. "Worry not about the

Netrocrians, Rygal. Our present issue is not with them, but with Kado, and with Safacon. Let us deal with them first."

Rygal looked up, a little surprised. "What do you know about Safacon, Iriam?"

Iriam nudged the tea kettle closer over the fire. "Little, I am afraid. I know he is no mere warlord. His powers match those of Norrin's, even exceed them, I think."

"He defeated the Guardians," Rygal said quietly, thinking. "I'm not sure Norrin would dare to challenge him again, even if he had the means." He thought of Norrin, of what had been lost—he knew Norrin still blamed himself for all that had happened, for all those who had fallen.

Llyrion and Dusty reappeared, with Tag following dutifully behind, and the discussion was left there. They all ate a hearty breakfast. Rygal felt rested, his stomach full of warm food, and he felt completely content to stay here for a long time, which was when Iriam spoke.

"We are going through the forest today," he said.

Rygal and Dusty looked up. Dusty frowned slightly. "Today? Why so soon?"

Iriam shook his head grimly. "Because the Hazes now know where you three are headed. Besides that, they are tracking you. I am not sure why. But they will assume you will go by the main road to get to Elimar—and in that case, that road will soon be guarded heavily."

Rygal's heart sank, and he felt a chill go down his spine as he pictured facing the Hazes again. "Then… we have to fight through?"

"There'd be too many of them," Llyrion said, looking at Iriam carefully. "Even for you."

"I know," Iriam said with a faint smile. "That is why we are not taking the main road."

Llyrion was studying the Neutral's face, and seemed to understand what this implied. His face fell in a look of dread. "No… we can't go that way… not with the children."

"Unless we face the Hazes, it is the only way in, Lieutenant," Iriam told him. "And you know we cannot risk the Hazes."

Rygal wasn't sure what they were talking about, but he was pretty sure he'd take anything over the Hazes. "How are we going through the forest?"

Iriam finally turned to look at them. "We are going through Grayline Swamp."

"Grayline Swamp?" Rygal repeated uncertainly. It was a chilly and gray morning—the idea of sloshing through a marsh was not particularly appealing. "We have to… walk through a marsh?"

"No, it is too deep to wade," Iriam said. "I have two small boats that we can use to get across."

"And we'll just hope that the Sirens aren't hungry," Llyrion muttered.

Dusty reacted at that, looking up at him quickly. "Sirens? There are Sirens in the swamp?" Her eyes were wide as she looked from Llyrion to Iriam.

Iriam, for once, looked a tiny bit guilty. "Well… yes, there are. If we go through the swamp around midday, most of them will be otherwise occupied. Besides that, I will be escorting you. They pose little threat compared to Hazes."

"*Otherwise occupied* as in *looking for a meal*," Llyrion said dryly.

Rygal was starting to feel left out again. "What… what are Sirens?"

Iriam looked at him. "Sirens are shape-shifters, hunters in the water, an amphibious race that use their powers to lure in their victims. They are excellent swimmers—their true form allows them to be very fast underwater."

"And we're sailing… in boats… over them," Dusty said haltingly. She was usually so eager to charge into danger that somehow her fear made Rygal uneasy too.

Iriam looked at her. "The Sirens will not attack as long as we remain in our boats. They will try to lure us into the water, but they will not attack. Stay in the boats, and you will be fine."

Rygal could see that neither Llyrion nor Dusty were fully convinced. Still, he knew they could trust Iriam. He had saved their lives, and offered shelter for the night. Now they would have to trust him again.

"Well, that's simple enough," he said out loud. "None of us want to go swimming anyway. If we stay in the boats, we'll probably be fine."

"Unless the Sirens are especially hungry," Dusty said worriedly.

Iriam looked at her. "I know this is hard, but you must trust me. This is the fastest way to Elimar, and we must avoid the Hazes."

A long silence. Finally Llyrion nodded. "Well, that's that, then. We'll go through Grayline."

......

The boats, as Rygal saw, were two lean, well-built canoes. They carried the two canoes across the clearing to a small dock that Iriam had built several years prior. As they prepared the boats, Rygal stared into the swamp. From initial appearance, it looked just like the forest, with tall trees and underbrush. But up close, he could see the miry water that had leaked in among the trees. The trees within the swamp were gray and dead, drowned in the water. A flood had come through many years before, Iriam had told them, and all the water had collected here. Brambles and briars had grown up on the dead trees, fencing the whole place in, and making it very dark.

The horses were another problem all together, as they quickly discovered. In the end, Iriam and Llyrion decided to load them onto a log raft that they could tow behind the canoes. The two horses balked nervously at the water's edge, but Llyrion managed to lead them on.

Iriam had Rygal ride in one canoe with Dusty, since Rygal had grown up around watercraft and could easily handle the oars. Rygal had only used canoes briefly—normally, he and Norrin used their sailboat. But it was fairly straightforward rowing, and the canoes moved swiftly and silently through the water.

"Stay close behind us," Iriam told them as he and Llyrion started off, towing the raft with the horses on board. "And remember—stay in your boat."

"Sit still, Tag," Dusty ordered the wolfhound, who was moving uncomfortably around on the canoe. Rygal dipped his paddle into the water and started after Iriam.

It was uncomfortably silent, the only sound coming from the soft sloshing of the paddles going in and out of the water, and the gentle rushing of the canoes as they moved along. Rygal showed Dusty how to paddle so that she could help. She was seated in the front of the canoe, looking around warily. Tag lay down behind her, his fur damp from the heavy mist, looking thoroughly miserable.

It was so unlike Dusty to be this nervous that it made Rygal worried too. "These Sirens," he asked her finally, "do they ever attack the Wildkids in Kasabren?"

Dusty shook her head, her eyes still scanning the swamp. "Well… these are a different kind. There's Black Sirens that cause trouble for us—they're huge. But they live in saltwater, and they're more animal-like. These ones here… they're smaller, at least from what Iriam's said."

"But you think they're still dangerous?" Rygal asked her, carefully maneuvering around a sunken log.

At that, Dusty nodded without hesitation. "They're Sirens.

They're smart, usually hungry, and they have no alliances with anyone."

"And… I'm guessing that's a bad thing," Rygal said slowly. He wasn't sure what the alliances part implied.

Dusty shrugged. "It means they can do whatever they want. They don't have to answer to anyone."

"Oh." Rygal paddled on, keeping an eye on the canoe in front of them.

Iriam looked calm as ever, which made Rygal a little calmer. Llyrion had one hand resting on his bow, an arrow nocked, ready to drop his paddle and shoot if any threat arose.

They had been rowing for most of the morning, and had seen nothing besides a few black squirrels and a snake on shore, when the first sound reached their ears. There was a splash, then, from the distance, came the sudden, unexpected sound of song.

Rygal's heart skipped a beat, but once his brain recognized the sound, he felt himself relax. It was…a woman, singing from somewhere in the swamp.

Now he saw her, seated on a half sunken log, looking lost to the world. Despite himself, he paused rowing. The woman was young, her face filled with bittersweet cheer, clad in a simple white gown. She was beautiful. As was her song, which seemed to penetrate into Rygal's very heart, making tears come to his eyes.

Why was she here, in this awful swamp? This wasn't safe for her…she should come with them. He could go to her and ask her to come along—

That was when a blast of ice shot out of Iriam's palm, crashing into the log the singer was seated on. Rygal opened his mouth to protest as the woman landed in the water, then stopped as his words caught in his throat. The woman fell into the water, surfaced, and gave a horrible gurgling snarl. Her face flattened, her head lengthened, and her form shrunk as she dove under the water.

"Sirens!" Iriam called from up ahead. "Keep close—and don't go to them, no matter what!"

Creatures churned the water around the boats. Rygal's heart was pounding. The Sirens weren't coming after them—just causing mischief enough to keep them tense and nervous. And it was working.

Tag was up and barking furiously. "Tag, down!" Dusty said sharply, scared and angry because of it.

A Siren reached up and gripped the side of the boat. Rygal saw its face, set in a bullet shaped head, a frill running down its spine. It had amber, cat-like eyes, a tiny nose, and a very wide mouth. It smiled hugely, showing sharp fangs.

"Come to play, little boy?" it asked, but its voice was the voice of the singing woman. Hearing that sweet voice come out of this monster was unsettling.

Dusty smacked at it with the paddle, and it ducked under water again, dodging. The paddle splashed into the water, and Dusty lurched forward, off balance. Then the clammy hand reached up again, grabbed her wrist, and pulled her straight down.

Dusty landed in the water with a splash. The canoe rocked violently. Rygal leaned over the side, peering into the murky water. "Dusty! Dusty!" His screams echoed around the swamp—he could hear Iriam calling something, a warning, but his focus was entirely on the place Dusty had disappeared.

Dusty surfaced a few feet to the right, gasping for breath. Rygal reached out for her, taking her hand, too relieved to realize what was happening. "Dusty—hold on—are you—"

His words stuck in his throat as Dusty's form disappeared before his eyes, changing back into what it truly was. The Siren smiled wickedly at him, then looked down at its paw, which Rygal was clutching. Before Rygal could let go, the Siren hauled him into the water.

Rygal could hear Tag's desperate barks from above as the Sirens dragged him and Dusty down.

# 11

## The King of the Sirens

Rygal hadn't even had time to take a breath. Now water pressed down on him, and his lungs screamed for air. The Siren had his arm in a tight grip, pulling him through the water. Rygal could see nothing except the blur of dark green around him. He thrashed desperately, but it was useless.

Then, suddenly, he felt himself dragged up on cold stone. Air reached his lips, and he inhaled deeply, then coughed. He was in a large stone cavern set just below the surface. The upper part of it was above water, but the entrance was under, like a beaver dam. Soaking wet and shivering, he pulled himself to a sitting position and looked around. There were Sirens everywhere, all of them smiling.

A Siren surfaced behind him, dragging Dusty up behind it. Rygal rushed to her. The Wildkid girl was very pale, and she didn't even seem to be breathing.

"Dusty," Rygal whispered hoarsely, horrified at the thought of losing his friend.

Then Dusty's eyes flew open, and she began coughing up all the swamp water she had swallowed. When she had caught her breath, she huddled next to Rygal. "Are you all right?" she whispered hoarsely.

"I'm fine," Rygal replied softly. "Don't be afraid. Iriam will come help us." He held her close, trying to warm both of them up.

The Siren that had pulled Rygal under now stretched luxuriously and yawned, showing its fangs. It was the first time Rygal had seen its whole body.

It looked a little like a very large newt, with a long body and short legs, but it had a frill going down the length of its back, and its neck was longer. Its eyes held a calculating intelligence as it studied the two captives. Its paws looked like human hands, although they only had four fingers, and in between the fingers was webbing. Its rear paws looked much the same, but longer and flatter than the front. The Siren studied them for a moment, then spoke, its voice quite human-like, though with a gentle rasp.

"Why come you?" it asked. Judging from its voice, it was male. Rygal saw that its frill was thick under its chin, like a beard, while some of the Sirens just had frills on their heads. So those must be females, and the male Sirens had full frills, he decided.

"We had to get to Elimar," Dusty said, glaring at the Siren.

"Why not main road?" the Siren inquired. Its Common Speech was broken and slow, and the slight accent confirmed Rygal's guess that the Sirens used their own language.

"We're being chased by Hazes," he said. "They're guarding the main road—that's why we had to go through your territory."

The assembled Sirens let out low, angry hisses at the mention of Hazes. That was a good sign—if they hated Kado too, maybe they would help.

"We're not here to fight you," Dusty added. "Please—will you please let us go?"

The Siren who had spoken turned and spoke briefly with the others in a swift, chattering language. They seemed to come to a decision. The first Siren turned to Rygal and Dusty again. "I be Kilas. I be deputy of Highness' army here. You will answer to King Sashan." He shouted out a command, and the Sirens encircled Dusty and Rygal, forcing them down a tunnel. It was pitch black, and very drippy. The stench of rotting vegetation—and other things— reached Rygal's nose, and he frowned.

"D'you think they'll eat us?" Dusty whispered. She sounded scared.

"I don't know," Rygal said. But he had a small feeling of hope. If the Sirens had wanted to eat them, they would have done it quickly and had it over with. But now they were being taken to their king. That was good, he figured—it was better than being eaten, anyway.

It was a long while of bumping along through the tunnel, with the Sirens whispering and occasionally laughing to themselves in the darkness around Rygal's knees. Then light came into view ahead. There was a tall cavern, with a perfectly round hole in the ceiling that let the moonlight stream through. A large fire burned in the center, making the whole place quite warm and well lit. After the darkness of the tunnel, this was welcoming.

Rygal and Dusty both moved subtly towards the fire to warm up while the Sirens spoke amongst themselves. Directly across the fire was a throne carved of limestone, and a Siren with green scales and yellow eyes sat upon it, wearing a golden crown. The Siren guards pushed Rygal and Dusty forward to stand before the throne.

Kilas bowed low. "King Sashan—we bring intruders from the eastern tunnel." Then he began speaking in the Siren tongue. Rygal hoped desperately that everything they said was good. There were many Sirens in the chamber, and many of them looked hungry.

The Siren King looked to Rygal now. "Is it true that you infiltrated our territory?" he asked, his voice slightly deeper than Kilas', and his Common a lot better.

"Yes…Your Highness," Rygal said slowly. He wasn't sure what to say.

The king, Sashan, studied him a moment. "Who are you?"

"I am Rygal of Gayrile," Rygal said carefully, "and this is Dusty, a Wildkid of Kasabren."

"I do not know those names," Sashan said shortly, eyes scanning them rapidly. "Gayrile I have heard of. But not of Wildkids."

"I—" Dusty started.

"I do not believe you to be a threat," Sashan said. "Why come you here?"

Rygal and Dusty exchanged a quick glance. The Sirens, evidently, knew of the Hazes, but where did they stand in this war? Clearly not with Kado…but probably not with the Liznees either…

"The roads are blocked," Rygal said finally. "The Hazes, Kado—they're trying to block the border."

"Why? Another petty fight among the two-legs is none of our interest," Sashan said flatly.

"It should be," Rygal boldly informed him. A few Sirens hissed; some in frustration, others in interest.

Sashan watched him. "Mind your tone, Rygal of Gayrile," he hissed softly.

Rygal took a breath. It would do no good to anger the Sirens, but they had to know the truth—and it was his and Dusty's best chance of getting out of here. "The Hazes. Kado has sent them to block the main roads, but that's not all. We're trying to get to Elimar, and Grayline Swamp is the quickest way since the roads aren't an option. But we also came here to… deliver a message."

"A message?" Sashan straightened slightly, looking interested.

Dusty looked at him in confusion, but Rygal pressed on. "Yes. A message from Dandio Ki."

That name caused interest. The Sirens may be unaffiliated with the Liznees, but everyone had heard of the heroic warrior. "What is this message?" Kilas asked.

"Kado is coming," Rygal said. "He's coming for everyone, for all of Coonsia, and don't think he'll stop there. If he defeats Caer Sia, he'll come here next. Your warriors, King Sashan, are the only real threat along the border—Kado's forces will come after you. And the Hazes won't be fooled by some songs and shape-shifting."

A long silence. Kilas glanced between the newcomers and the king.

Sashan straightened. "We know of the Hazes, and of Kado. They have killed many of my warriors already. We cannot risk a battle with them."

"You won't have to fight them," Rygal said, taking a breath. "We're going to do that for you. But… until that time arrives, your people will want to be below ground, out of the sight of the Hazes."

"As we let them walk all over our lands?" Sashan hissed.

"I don't think they'll get this far. We plan to hold them at Caer Sia. But in case they should, you need to be in hiding. All of you." Rygal paused. "And you'll have to let us go to do that."

Sashan studied him. "Indeed. But how do I know you are not with Kado yourself, when you reek of Haze?"

A tense silence followed the words—there was nothing Rygal could say to deny that, and all the Sirens looked suspicious. "I'm not," Rygal stammered, thrown off guard by the question. "We aren't—"

A voice, wonderfully familiar, spoke from the end of the chamber. "They are with me, Sashan," said Iriam, standing tall in the darkness. "They are not with Kado."

"Iriam!" Dusty said in relief. The Neutral nodded briefly to them, but his eyes were on the Siren King.

Most of the assembled Sirens nodded and made room for Iriam. Clearly the Neutral was a respected figure in this part of the country.

Sashan looked uncertain but no longer suspicious. "With you? And what is their purpose here?"

"They are riding to Elimar. I offered them passage through the forest," Iriam explained. "They have been sent by Sia itself—Dandio Ki sent them."

Rygal let out a pent-up breath. Iriam could not have confirmed Rygal's story better than if he'd been in on the whole thing.

Sashan thought a moment. "In this case, then you may claim them. You may pass through the swamp."

Iriam bowed slightly in thanks. "Thank you, sire. And you would do well to heed the boy's warning. Allow the Liznees to deal with the Hazes. You must remain here, out of the way of the battle." He turned, his black cloak billowing behind him as he led the two of them out of the cavern.

"I am glad to see you both are all right," Iriam said as they left. "Sashan's people are not always kind to strangers, not in these times."

"But if they know you, why did they attack us at first?" Dusty asked.

"Bored, I assume," Iriam said as he led them up the slippery steps that led up above ground. "And we came as they awoke from their noon time rest. They might have been hungry too."

Dusty looked at Rygal. "What in the world was all that about Dandio sending us to give a message? And warning them not to attack the Hazes? The Sirens might actually have a chance against them."

"You know they wouldn't," Rygal told her, shaking his head. "I don't know. I guess… I figured they would listen, and not eat us."

"You did well," Iriam told him. "Whether or not Sashan chooses to listen will be up to him. You gave them ample warning, and I hope they will heed it. It was quick thinking."

Coming from Iriam, this was the best praise Rygal could hope for. Llyrion was waiting on shore with the horses. A little path led through the forest, winding and small but better than more swamp. He was relieved to see them, and Rygal and Dusty quickly explained what had happened.

It was late afternoon, and the sun shone through the trees. Iriam looked back across the swamp, satisfied. "There, that was not so bad, was it?"

The others managed to laugh.

Iriam tied the canoes together and looked back across the swamp. "I must return home now. With the Hazes so close, I must make sure that the Sirens stay hidden, to avoid any unnecessary battle." Rygal felt a stab of sorrow at losing Iriam, with his leadership and calm confidence. "The border is only a few miles away," Iriam continued. "You should reach Elimar by nightfall."

"Thank you," Llyrion said, and Rygal and Dusty echoed him.

Iriam nodded simply. "I am glad to have helped you. Now,

remember your mission, and do not give up. May the High Light guard your steps."

"And yours," Llyrion said, as the Neutral started paddling back across the water. He turned back briefly, and Rygal saw him raise a hand in parting, ice shimmering on his fingertips.

# 12

## Elimar in Early Winter

Llyrion insisted that Rygal and Dusty get some rest before they move on. Both of them were still soaking wet, and now that they were out of the humid swamp, they were quite chilled. They wrapped themselves in dry cloaks and took a quick rest. Llyrion woke them an hour later, and they mounted up and continued riding west.

"Will Iriam come to help us in the battle, do you think?" Dusty asked as they started riding.

Llyrion glanced back at her. "He may. But I wouldn't hope too highly."

"He's allied with the Liznees—of course he'll help us," Rygal said. "Right?"

"Well, that's true. Honestly, I'm not sure. Iriam is allied with the Liznees, yes, but… well, that's not really the right word. He chooses to help us." Llyrion's brow wrinkled in thought. "He's a Neutral, a Netrocrian… he thinks in different ways, I suppose. More likely he will come in the aftermath."

The land changed after leaving the swamp. The trees, which had before been elegant birches and maples, slowly changed to tall firs and pines. Birdsong filled the early evening, and an owl hooted deep in the forest. Soon they came to a river, flowing fast and churning into a froth.

"This is the Hallas," Llyrion said. "The natural border of Daffodalion. This means we are officially in Coonsia."

They crossed the weather-worn bridge, and Rygal felt a stir of excitement. They had reached Coonsia. Daffodalion was behind them, and this meant that Caer Sia was only a few day's ride north. He looked to his right, north, and could see the tall peaks of the Diamond Cap mountain range, illuminated by the evening light. In that valley lay Caer Sia.

The trail became wider once they crossed the bridge, better traveled. The horses moved at a brisk trot, as though sensing that their journey was nearing an end. Tag followed, pausing every now and then to sniff a fern or branch.

Elimar finally came into view. Lampposts lit the roads in the early evening, casting a golden light on the cluster of homes on the outskirts of town. More lights shone in the distance, near the center of town. The houses and buildings became closer compacted there, the shops taller and better built. Rygal could see the dome of the City Hall above the houses.

The Elves of Elimar weren't ruled by a duke or lord, as was common with many Coonsian cities. Rather, they operated under a council of five, who governed any Elven happenings in this part of Coonsia.

"Where will we stay tonight, Llyrion?" Dusty asked.

"With my family—my father's house, with my wife and son. We'll be there in a minute," Llyrion told her, leading them down a side street, then another.

They moved along the dirt road, past farmhouses and simple cottages. The musty smell of farm animals and damp soil filled the air.

Llyrion's eyes scanned the houses along the road, then he reined up and dismounted. The house before them was an old farmhouse, with a thatch roof and a flower bed in the front. The flower beds were well tended, with a few flowers still clinging to their stalks in defiance of winter's coming.

A tall Elf stood on the porch, holding a lantern. "Good evening," he called out as the three companions approached.

Llyrion's tired face broke into a smile as he stepped forward. "Father! I thank you for waiting for us. We were delayed a little on the journey."

"So I guessed, and I am very glad to see you alive," the man said, moving forward and meeting them on the road.

Rygal and Dusty dismounted stiffly. Tag had already rushed forward, his tail wagging in a slow rhythm. The tall Elf knelt and let the young wolfhound sniff him before fondling his ears. Tag's tail wagged faster—he could tell a dog lover when he saw one.

The stranger stood again and clasped Llyrion's hand in greeting, and Llyrion turned as the other two approached. "Rygal, Dusty, this is my father, Llio. And Father, this is Rygal of Gayrile and Dusty of Kasabren, companions of Dandio Ki."

Llio shook their hands in turn, smiling. He had the same chiseled features, friendly face, and twinkling eyes as his son. His hair was chin length, and had once been the same reddish-blond as Llyrion's, but had by now faded into silver. "Ah, it is good to meet you both. I'm glad to see you all made it here safe, in these dark times."

"Well, we certainly have a story to share," Llyrion told him tiredly.

Llio led them into the house. "Well, come in, and we can hear it over dinner. I assume you're all hungry."

The three of them nodded hopefully and followed him inside. Llyrion's home was not especially large, but quite tidy. Stairs led up to the bedrooms on the second story. A kitchen was to the right of the doorway, and to the left was a parlor, where a fire crackled merrily on the hearth.

Two figures emerged from the parlor as they entered, a slender and elegant Elven woman and a small boy who looked to be around six or seven. Llyrion embraced them both, then introduced them as his wife Linwy and son Alder.

"It is good to meet you both," Linwy said, smiling at Rygal and Dusty. Her hair was long and dark, pulled back into a simple but stylish braid. Her eyes were blue and had the sort of kind sparkle that mothers tend to have.

Once the three of them had washed up, they settled down around the table for dinner, which turned out to be a savory beef stew with home-made bread.

Rygal ate hungrily, only pausing every now and then to nod in answer to a question. Llyrion told the story of meeting up with Dandio in the forest, facing off with the Hazes, meeting Iriam, and the encounter with the Sirens.

"Ah, so Iriam still guards those parts," Llio said with interest. "I am glad to hear it. Perhaps he can hold Kado back for a while."

"I hope so," Llyrion agreed.

After dinner, Linwy led Dusty and Rygal upstairs for bed. After setting Dusty up in one room, she nodded to another. "I put a spare tunic in there for you, so leave your wet clothes by the door and I can wash them," she told him.

"Thanks," Rygal said, stifling a yawn. It was the first real bed he'd slept in since leaving Gayrile, and suddenly he realized how long that had been, and how tired he was. He changed, left his dirty clothes in the hall like Linwy had instructed, and flopped down.

It had been a long day. Despite the questions and thoughts swarming Rygal's head, he soon fell asleep.

. . . . . .

Morning dawned bright and sunny. Rygal slowly came out of dreams, blinking in the light that streamed in under the curtains. A pleasant smell was coming from downstairs, making his mouth water.

He sat up. There were a fresh set of clothes hanging on the door, and he dressed quickly. The shirt and pants were a little too big, but they were a welcome change after his tattered ones. As he laced up the boots Dandio had given him, his mind wandered to Gayrile, and he wondered how Norrin was doing. Winter was fast approaching. Rygal hoped he'd be home again before the first snow.

He jogged downstairs. Linwy stood in the kitchen, working over the wood stove. The pleasant smell of baked pastry rose in the air.

"Good morning," the Elven woman said with a smile. "Breakfast will be ready in a little while. Dusty has taken Tag outside."

Rygal nodded, rubbing sleep from his eyes. The sun shone through the window, making the frosty grass glisten.

Dusty entered through the front door, with Alder at her heels, both of them talking to Tag. "Down, boy," Dusty said quickly as Tag, seeing Rygal, trotted forward, tail wagging, trying to stand up and lick his face. Rygal pushed him down, patting his head.

"He likes watching the chickens," Dusty observed to Rygal, plopping down in a chair.

"Can we get a dog, Mum?" Alder asked hopefully.

Linwy raised her eyebrows. "A dog? He's practically a wolf." She nodded at Tag.

"We don't have sheep," Alder pointed out, as though that were the only reason for his mother to object. "Besides, he could help us protect the other animals."

Linwy smiled at her eager son. "Well, I won't say no right away. Still, why don't you enjoy your friends while they're here, and then talk to your father about it later."

Alder seemed satisfied, and sat on the floor as Tag bounded over to him.

Llio and Llyrion came in a few more minutes later, and they enjoyed a meal of ham and baked sweet rolls with jam. When they had finished, Rygal finally asked the question that weighed on him.

"What's our plan now, Llyrion?"

Llyrion thought for a moment. "My task was to rally the Elves against Kado; in all likelihood I'll spend a bit of time at City Hall today." His smile faded slightly at this. While it was a noble cause, there was nothing especially appealing about spending a day persuading the rather pompous leaders to help.

"Might want a bit of help with that then, I'd imagine?" Llio asked, arching an eyebrow.

"Maybe," Llyrion said, looking hopefully at the older man.

Llio nodded. "Well, I'll come with you. Maybe two witnesses will speed the whole process." His son smiled and nodded.

"Then what should we do, while you're gone?" Dusty asked.

Rygal was pretty sure he knew the answer. "Stay here," Llyrion said. "You've been traveling hard for days—you should enjoy this break while it lasts. Dandio and Glentree will hopefully be here tomorrow or the day after, and then you'll be traveling again—no, enjoy this while you can."

"All right," Rygal said, slightly disappointed. "But—couldn't I come to City Hall and help you? I mean, I've seen the Hazes too, and I could help persuade the council, maybe."

"I'm sure you could, but unfortunately our people take little heed of strangers," Llyrion said with a wry smile. "Especially young ones. I appreciate the offer, Rygal, but I don't think it'd do much good."

"All right," Rygal said again, defeated.

The day passed slowly, which was made worse by his curiosity. Llyrion and Llio left for City Hall an hour or so after breakfast, and Rygal guessed he wouldn't see them till later in the day.

Linwy, thankfully, sensed his boredom and put him to work. There were many tasks to be done around the farm and the house, and Rygal and Dusty were both bored enough to accept willingly. Rygal shoveled stalls, milked the two cows, and cleaned out the chicken pens. By the time evening approached, he felt exhausted, and gratefully accepted a warm bath.

He finished, changed into clean clothes, and headed out into the parlor, waiting. Alder sat down by him, looking at him curiously. "What did it feel like?" the young boy asked unexpectedly.

Rygal looked at him, confused. "What did what feel like?"

"When you almost turned into one of the—one of the creatures," Alder said slowly. "Dusty said it happened fast, and that she was scared. She didn't want to tell me any more." He looked at Rygal, half-fearfully, as though he expected Rygal to transform before his eyes.

"I…" Rygal thought a moment, a little confused. "It hurt, I guess. I don't remember it very well. It's all kinda… blurry. Like trying to remember a bad dream." He shrugged, not sure how to put it into words.

The young Elf seemed to consider this, then nodded slightly, stood and left the room.

It was warm in the house, with the fire stoked to keep out the chill night air. Somehow, it felt too hot, and Rygal got up and stood on the porch, watching as dusk fell. He thought of the Hazes, of Kado, and how there may possibly be a way to turn them back.

He thought of Llyrion as he thought of that. The Elf's reaction when talking about helping the Hazes meant something, Rygal knew. He wondered if it was because Llyrion knew someone who had been turned into a Haze… someone important to him. Maybe that was why Llyrion was so determined to figure it out. Maybe that was why he didn't want to talk about it…

His shoulder was aching dimly, and he rubbed it distractedly. By now, everyone in his town would know he was gone. Most everyone— Mr. Kellis, the Morris boys—had probably given up hope.

Had Norrin?

Rygal swallowed. Norrin might have given up hope that he was alive. Maybe he had—

No. He shook his head. No, Norrin would never forget him. And Rygal was pretty sure that Norrin would still be holding out hope that he was alive.

He also remembered that he finally had access to a postal service here, which made his heart lift a little. That meant he could send a letter letting Norrin know that he was here and alive—he'd have to do that tomorrow.

He turned to go back into the house, noticing that his shoulder was really hurting him. That was odd. The wound didn't normally hurt like this. Unless…

A sound.

Rygal looked up, his eyes scanning the darkness, his heart pounding. Some noise had reached his ears, faint, but there. At the same time, the pain in his shoulder faded.

Maybe he had just imagined it…maybe his confused mind had imagined it on its own. But…

Rygal took a step forward, onto the road, looking down the way that led from the border. Nothing.

He had just started to go back inside when the sound of horse hooves came to his ears, and he turned swiftly.

An elegant black horse rounded the corner, her head lowered. The mare froze as she saw Rygal, then let out a low whinny. She was limping, Rygal realized, and her saddle was empty. He started towards the horse, a little confused and worried. Then, as he reached her, his heart almost stopped.

There was fresh blood staining the saddle, and not the horse's blood either. And as he drew close, he recognized the black horse before him, even before he saw the symbol on the saddle blanket, a symbol he knew as the crest of the house of the Liznees.

It was Dandio's horse before him.

And Dandio himself was nowhere to be seen.

# 13

## A Rider in the Night

Rygal stared at the horse in blank shock for a moment, the blood in the saddle making him feel sick. The mare snorted softly, a little uneasy, still favoring her left hind leg. There was no sign of a wound—in all likelihood she had pulled a muscle or ligament in her frantic gallop.

Where was Dandio?

Rygal didn't think to lead the horse inside, or run back inside to get help—he ran down the road in the direction the horse had come. He could see well enough in the dim light, enough not to trip over something, anyway. His mind was racing and dread was filling him. Dandio's horse, alone, with blood staining the saddle, injured after a long run or a fight—but what had happened?

He tripped over a tree root that had overgrown into the path. This was probably a blessing in disguise, because he would never have seen Dandio if he hadn't fallen and happened to glance at the tree.

Dandio was leaning, back against the tree, slumped in the shadows just off the road. His eyes were half-closed, his breathing faint.

"Dandio!"

Rygal knelt by him, fear rising inside him, trying to assess any injuries. In the faint light, it was difficult to see. As his eyes adjusted, his stomach twisted as he saw the wound running down the Liznee's arm, a long, cruel gash weeping blood into the underbrush. But while that was the source of blood, it didn't seem to be the principle injury. There was a dark bruise near Dandio's temple, made from a blow from some blunted object. He was wavering between waking and total unconsciousness.

Rygal studied both injuries uncertainly, not sure what to do. There was no way he could move the Liznee down the road—he would only worsen the wounds. Dandio needed medical attention.

In the same moment, he realized that he couldn't leave him here. Dandio had information, that much he was sure. He had tried to get back to Elimar—probably to find them and pass on the news. If word got out that Dandio Ki was staying in Elimar's public hospital, there was no telling what would happen. Kado might come and—

Dandio's eyes flickered, and he muttered something faintly. His gaze settled on Rygal. "Rygal?" he said weakly, confusion crossing his face. He tried to sit up, then winced and sat down again.

"I'm here," Rygal said, gripping his hand. "What—"

"Orcs," Dandio managed to gasp. "Many of them, on the road between here and the border. I think—I think they have sided with Kado."

Rygal felt a tremor of fear, but at the same time, relief. At least the weapon that had hurt Dandio wasn't one of the Hazes' enchanted blades. He remembered the ache in his wound a few moments before Dandio's horse had come into view, and assumed that the Hazes must have been working with the orcs.

"Are you all right?" he asked worriedly. Dandio's wounds looked serious. But Rygal couldn't just leave him here.

"I've taken worse," Dandio said with a faint smile. "Glad to see… you made it here. I think…" he trailed off and coughed.

"Can you stand? What happened?" Rygal stammered. Dandio and Glentree weren't supposed to be back in Elimar for at least another day—for Dandio to turn up, alone, could mean nothing good.

Dandio coughed again, his voice growing fainter. "News… about the Hazes. For Llyrion. About his brother…"

Rygal looked at him, confused, not sure if Dandio's concussed mind was telling the truth or was confusing the situation. "His… brother?" Suddenly, the pieces fell in place—Llyrion's determination to free the Hazes, the sorrow on his face when he spoke of their plight—

It was beginning to spit rain. Rygal huddled under the tree, his mind working through the situation. He couldn't carry Dandio back to the farm. He definitely couldn't leave him here either though.

There was nothing for it. They would have to wait.

. . . . . .

Dusty had finished playing with Tag and Alder, and now both the little boy and the wolf pup were fast asleep. She smiled, then turned to Linwy.

"Do you think we have any chance against the Hazes?" she asked, concern and curiosity in her voice.

Linwy gave her a comforting smile. "Don't worry. I am sure that the High Light will protect us."

Dusty nodded thoughtfully, then looked outside. "It's raining. Where's Rygal?"

She opened the front door and looked out. No sign. Puzzled, she started to turn around when a horse trotted down the front path, riderless and favoring one leg.

"Linwy!" Dusty stepped out into the rain, moving to the injured horse. She stroked the soft muzzle, and then froze as the light fell on the symbol embroidered on the saddle blanket. This was Dandio's horse…and on the saddle, staining it—something red.

Blood.

"What is it?" Linwy asked, glancing out the door. Seeing the horse, she frowned slightly, moving forward. "Hello—where did she come from?"

Dusty took a shaking breath, then the words tumbled out of her. "This—this is Dandio's horse—she's hurt, and there's blood in the saddle—I think—I think—" She couldn't finish. If Dandio had been killed or injured, had Rygal gone to find him? Or… had he been captured by whoever attacked Dandio?

Both of them looked down the road, through the rain, in the growing darkness.

Then Linwy turned, a determined look in her eyes. "Tether the horse there. I'll fetch a lantern."

"Linwy—where should we look?" Dusty looked around, feeling overwhelmed. In the growing darkness, if Dandio or Rygal was injured or unable to respond to their calls—it could take all night to find them.

Linwy took her shoulders, her eyes piercing into the young Wildkid's. "Listen to me. You are a Wildkid. Your senses, they are higher attuned than mine. You must listen, scent the wind, pick up any clues for him. It's our only chance."

Dusty took a calming breath and listened. She could hear the pattering rain, the soft breeze in the forest beyond, the pounding of her own heart. The breeze blew close to her face, carrying a jumble of confusing scents. Then, one of them was familiar. Rygal. She could distinguish that scent now, mixed with fear and adrenaline and the faint bitter scent of blood—

Her ears picked up the faint sounds that only a Wildkid could hear, distant but there. She turned to Linwy, feeling her confidence grow, and they started down the road.

. . . . . .

The rain intensified slightly, and Rygal shifted to be more sheltered by the tree's boughs. They had huddled here for twenty minutes, but it felt like longer. Dandio lay silent, eyes open and alert.

"There are orcs coming," he said suddenly, his voice soft.

Rygal looked at him sharply. He wasn't sure if Dandio was thinking straight, but at the same time he could hear a faint sound in the trees beyond, the cracking of branches and underbrush of someone trying to move quietly but failing badly.

"Orcs?" he whispered, his mouth dry.

Dandio's eyes, which had been clouded slightly when Rygal had first found him, were clear. His face was quite serious. "You hear them?"

Rygal listened. The distant cracking sounds were growing louder. He hoped, for one wild moment, that it was Dusty or Linwy or Llyrion coming to save them. But even as he thought this, he saw a glimpse of one of them, moving through the trees.

He had never seen an orc before. The creatures moving through the woods, barely twenty paces from them, moved in a slow, hunched motion, almost like a bear. Their faces were box-like, the jaws wider and longer than a human's, with the teeth coming up over the upper lip. Their ears were pig-like, their eyes small and dark. They wore primitive but clearly effective armor.

"How many?" Dandio asked softly. He seemed remarkably calm.

"Nine," Rygal whispered back. He realized he had, without thinking, been counting the creatures as they emerged.

Dandio muttered something under his breath, then straightened painfully, getting stiffly to his knees.

"What are you doing?" Rygal hissed, paralyzed with fear at the thought of being found. "They'll see!"

"They already see us, or smell us, at any rate," Dandio said wearily. He was right—the orcs were moving slowly towards their position. Rygal froze, heart pounding. They were badly outnumbered, Dandio was injured, and he didn't have a sword or even know how to fight—

The lead orc stopped, five paces from them. It held a heavy spear. Despite its lurching gait, Rygal could tell that it knew how to use it. Its eyes scanned the two figures briefly, then it grunted, "Daffonic?"

"Common," Dandio said slowly. The orc's animal-like brow furrowed.

"Lizn'ean," it grunted, the word slightly garbled.

"*Narti,*" Dandio murmured, sounding like they had come to an agreement on what language they would converse in. They spoke in a flowing language that Rygal didn't recognize, though he guessed it was the Liznee tongue. The orc sounded more confused than angry, which seemed like a good sign. Dandio responded in the same tongue, his voice still calm and level. He had got to his feet, leaning against the tree, a hand on his knife hilt.

The two of them conversed for a few tense seconds. The orc seemed uneasy, standing stiff and clutching the spear—Dandio still seemed calm.

Finally, the orc grunted and nodded, turning back and grunting to the others. Slowly, the other orcs turned and faded back into the trees.

"Rygal?"

Rygal turned, startled by the familiar voice. Dusty was calling, somewhere in the trees—

"We're here," he called, his voice cracking—the strain of the last few minutes made him feel like a tense mass of nerves.

Dandio slid down the tree trunk, his face pale. Rygal stumbled out onto the road, his eyes seeing the welcome light of a lantern. Dusty and Linwy were walking toward them, looking worried.

"We're here," Rygal told them. "Dandio's here, hurry…"

"What happened? I could hear something—it didn't sound—it didn't sound friendly," Dusty stammered, her face fearful.

"Must have been the orc…"

"Orcs?" Linwy repeated, staring at him in disbelief and worry. "There were orcs here?"

"Dandio talked to them and they left—I'm not sure what happened…" Rygal trailed off, knowing they would get very little information from Dandio tonight. He was barely conscious—talking to the orc seemed to have taken the last of his energy.

Together, Rygal and Linwy managed to support the injured Liznee between them as they slowly walked back to the house. It was still raining, a steady, soaking drizzle that had them wet and shivering by the time they reached the house. Rygal glanced back into the darkening evening. The dark was good, he decided. The last thing they needed was a group of confused Elves pounding on Llyrion's door the next morning. In all likelihood no one had seen them.

They lowered Dandio onto the couch. He was awake now, and looked less pale, but he winced at the pain as Linwy set to work on his bleeding arm. The Elven woman, it seemed, had some knowledge of medicine, and was working rapidly to assess the wound.

She set a warm wet rag on the wound, then turned to Rygal. "Are you hurt?"

"I'm fine," Rygal said, his eyes never leaving Dandio's face. "The orcs—will he—"

"He will live," Linwy said with a tired smile. "The wounds will mend."

Rygal glanced outside, his mind going back to the orcs. "Will they—will they come back?"

"They shouldn't," Dandio said hoarsely, raising his head weakly. "Those ones—they weren't the ones that attacked me—they were tribal members, coming down south to investigate Kado's army. They're neutral… as far as I can tell."

Rygal relaxed, and suddenly felt very tired, and wet, and cold. Linwy seemed to sense this, and looked up at him. "You should go rest. We'll discuss all this in the morning."

Rygal nodded tiredly and started up the steps. Dusty ran after him, catching up. "What happened to him?"

"Orcs, apparently," Rygal said tiredly. "Probably that border patrol Llyrion was trying to avoid before we met Iriam."

"But why is he here in the first place? I thought he and Glentree are in the Southern Fiefs, and travel here tomorrow—and where is Glentree?" Dusty's face was worried.

Rygal hadn't thought of that, and now felt a new stir of unease. But he knew there would be no telling until tomorrow.

. . . . . .

The following morning everyone still felt on edge. Linwy had told yesterday's events to Llio and Llyrion, who had returned late last night, and that left everyone waiting expectantly to hear why Dandio was here.

For his part, Dandio was doing better. The head injury, coupled with sheer exhaustion, had left him weakened. But he was clearly stronger than last night, and joined the others around the table for breakfast. He thanked Linwy multiple times for her help, as well as thanking Rygal and Dusty the moment they appeared downstairs.

"I wasn't sure I would be able to find you—any of you," Dandio admitted as they ate. "After I fell from the saddle, I was sure I would have to wait out the night and hobble into town the next day. You have my thanks," he said to Rygal, smiling.

Rygal blushed, but he felt a warm glow of satisfaction. He set down his plate and looked up at Dandio carefully. "How are you doing?" There was a bandage around Dandio's arm, and a dark bruise colored his temple.

But the Liznee only smiled. "Better. I'll be fine."

Dusty turned to Dandio. "Well, now that we're all here, will you tell us? What happened last night?"

Everyone looked at Dandio expectantly.

Dandio took a breath. The smile had faded from his face.

"Well… that's a bit of a story," he said finally. "After you left with Llyrion, Glentree and I continued to the Southern Fiefs. Two of them agreed to help fight against Kado. The other two were… a different matter."

A worried silence fell over the table. "What happened?" Llyrion asked slowly.

Dandio looked up. "The other two southern fiefs have pledged alliance with Kado. He has offered them substantial reward, in exchange for more troops. His army has at least doubled in size now, by my guess. Glentree and I barely escaped with our lives."

"What could Kado possibly want with Coonsian soldiers, though?" Rygal asked finally, slightly confused. "I mean… he has the Hazes, and they're unstoppable—well, unless you're Iriam."

"A warlord always has need for new troops," Dandio pointed out. "Besides that, I doubt Kado would let them remain… as they are, if you understand my meaning."

"He's going to turn them… into Hazes?" Llyrion guessed.

"I don't doubt it," Dandio said quietly. "The duke of the town neighboring the two that turned traitor told us that the soldiers there have been promised great power and strength. And who do we know who likes making powerful, strong, and brainwashed soldiers?"

"Kado," Dusty said softly.

Rygal looked up at Dandio, studying the Liznee's face carefully. For the weight of this news, and the weariness from the long ride and last night, he seemed surprisingly… optimistic. Hopeful even. Rygal could see that green spark of determination in his eyes. "So why do you look so…unworried about this?" he asked.

Dandio looked up, and the trace of a smile crossed his battered features. "Because we know how to turn the Hazes back."

# 14

## The Scheme of Kado

Everyone responded at once. Llyrion sat bolt upright, a glimmer of hope coming back into his tired eyes. "You what? How? Where did you find out?"

"When did you find out?" Dusty asked.

"Was the trick in the timing, like we thought?" That was Llyrion again, hardly able to stay in his seat, his face earnest.

Dandio raised his hands, motioning for quiet. "All right, all right, settle down and I'll tell you the whole story."

Silence fell abruptly as they all waited anxiously.

Dandio took a breath. "Glentree and I left the southern fiefs and began traveling north like we had planned. We carried the dire news of the two fiefs betraying us, news that the High King needed to know of quickly. We were also looking for an old ally, the Neutral Iriam."

"We met him!" Rygal interrupted eagerly. "We met him and he saved us from the Hazes."

Dandio nodded. "Yes, well, we couldn't make contact with him. Later, I realized this was because of the blockade along the roads. Glentree and I ended up camping near the border, to the south of the Siren lands. And that's when the Haze came."

"Just one?" Dusty said, at the same time that Llyrion slid back in his seat, his face suddenly pale.

"Just one," Dandio said, staring grimly at the table top. He paused briefly, then continued. "The Haze looked just like most of the others, but there was something different about it. It was stumbling and trying to get toward us. By this point Glentree and I both had our weapons ready, but it wasn't trying to attack."

He hesitated again, trying to decide how to explain it. The others waited breathlessly. Llyrion sat stiffly, listening, his face drawn and tense.

"The Haze fell on its knees a few paces from us. By then Glentree and I had realized that it wasn't trying to attack—nor did it seem, in any way, that it had been sent from Kado. It was resisting the spell."

"Resisting?" Rygal repeated, startled. He knew the Hazes were blind and deaf to everything but Kado's wishes. The fact that one could have broken that hold enough to even consider resisting was stunning.

Unless…

"Wait… you think it was remembering its past?" he guessed.

"I think that might have been going through its head," Dandio said. "It's hard to say. But it was trying to speak—it said something about Kado, and then mentioned the High King. And… well, it's hard to explain. The best I can explain it is imagine a window, covered in steam or fog, slowly clearing. That's what it looked like. The Haze was changing back—with every question that Glentree and I asked, it was turning back."

He looked up at Llyrion, hesitating a moment. "It was Lorell."

Rygal didn't recognize this name, but the entire Tarash family reacted. Linwy gasped and put a hand to her mouth, Llio looked up sharply and moved closer to Dandio. Only Llyrion was silent, and nodded very slowly. His face was pale and drawn.

"Who's…" Rygal started slowly, sensing no one would tell him otherwise.

Llyrion spoke, his voice strained. "Lorell Tarash was my brother. Taken by Kado, transformed into a Haze about a month ago. We were out riding together—the Hazes caught us. He let himself be taken to let me escape." His face was calm, but his voice trembled slightly.

Rygal looked back to Dandio, slowly putting the implication of this together. "How'd he remember?"

"He was the Haze that injured you, Rygal. Apparently, he was also one of the ones that attacked you three before Iriam saved you," Dandio said. "He explained a little of it—when he saw you alive, and not transformed, it broke Kado's hold. Briefly, but effectively. He remembered his life, fragments of it. He saw Llyrion his brother, and remembered Elimar.

"He went south after that, weakening, but driven by determination. Someone had to help him escape Kado's hold. He found us, and we managed to help him remember. And that broke the spell." Dandio paused again, looking at Llyrion.

Llyrion looked up slowly, and smiled slightly. It was a sad sort of smile. "He died, didn't he? The strain of it was too great?"

"I don't think it was the strain," Dandio said slowly. "He had been injured. Some of the orcs tracked him after he left the Hazes and shot at him. The extra strength of returning to himself was too much."

Llyrion nodded and looked down at his hands. Linwy moved behind him, placing her hands on her husband's shoulders and resting her brow on the top of his head.

There was a long silence. Somehow, they all knew there were no words to ease the pain.

Dusty looked at Dandio. "So… the way to save the Hazes… we have to help them remember? But I thought you said that wouldn't work."

"And I don't think it would, originally," Dandio said. "But the seed has been sown. Lorell, even at the end, knew that much. If he had not been dying he could have told us a lot more. He did manage to convey that Kado's hold on the Hazes is weakening. Kado's concern has become more for quantity than for quality. The more and more troops he creates, the more he has to control, and that is growing more difficult."

"Then why not just kill Kado?" Rygal said. "I mean—if he's the one controlling all this, then killing him would be a lot easier."

But Dandio shook his head. "That's not how it works. If Kado were dead, the shock of it would probably cause a lot more damage than good. The Hazes have been completely dependent on him from the start. If his voice was abruptly silenced in their heads, who knows what could happen. They might all die. Or they might turn on Caer Sia in a blind rage and destroy everything. They wouldn't be healed, just enraged and lost."

"It has to be their choice," Llyrion said, his voice slightly rasping. He cleared his throat. "It has to be their decision—just like how Rygal fought back against Kado's voice and remembered Gayrile despite of it. We'll just be there to help them. Like Dandio was for Lorell."

Dandio nodded. "Yes. We buried Lorell near the border. I will show you the place after this is all over," he added to Llyrion, who nodded his thanks. "Glentree and I split ways. He needed to get to Caer Sia before the snow blocked the pass, and I needed to bring the news to Elimar. I didn't remember the orcs along the border—too late, unfortunately. I fought through them—one of them slashed down my arm, and another clubbed me just as I was escaping. I managed to hold on until we reached the main road outside of Elimar—I remember falling from the saddle, and after that, nothing, until Rygal found me."

There was a brief silence.

"Then what will we do now?" Rygal asked.

Dandio straightened. "We ride to Badwater, and then sail east to Caer Sia."

"We won't ride?" Dusty asked, a little disappointed.

Dandio shook his head. "By now the mountain passes will be blocked with snow. All that rain yesterday—there'll be snow in the mountains. I just hope Glentree made it through." He chewed his lip, looking worried.

"If anyone could get through, it'd be Glentree," Llyrion pointed out with a weak smile.

Dandio nodded slightly, looking at him. "What do you plan to do?"

Llyrion shrugged very slightly. The grief of losing his brother was weighing heavily on him, Rygal could see. "Whatever you want me to do. I'm prepared to ride to Badwater with you—Kado must be brought to justice."

But Dandio shook his head. "No. Stay here. Stay with your family. We will deal with Kado."

"And the Hazes?" Llyrion asked, arching an eyebrow. "Please, Dandio. After all this time, I'm ready to help stop them. Let me avenge Lorell."

Dandio hesitated only for a moment longer, then nodded. "Very well." He stood, glancing at Rygal and Dusty. "Best go gather your things. It's quite a ride to Badwater."

# 15

## The Sun's Crest

The ride northwest to Badwater was a long one, but thankfully uneventful. They left Elimar, with thanks to Llyrion's family for sheltering them, and then rode north. By nightfall, the weather had only grown colder, and Rygal was chilled to the bone by morning. Dandio woke them just after sunrise, and they set off again after a short meal. As they rode north, the rain turned into a gentle snow.

It was late afternoon by the time the sound of the sea came to Rygal's ears, bringing a salty scent. Somehow, he felt content. The sea was a place he was used to, a place he had grown up by. He squinted north, across the waters, wishing he could somehow see Gayrile, where he hoped Norrin waited.

"We're nearly there," Dandio said, sliding from his saddle.

Llyrion had dismounted as well. "I'll head into town and buy us passage onto the first ship headed to Sia. It won't be a moment." And with that he pulled his hood over his head and moved toward town.

Tag looked to be enjoying the chilly weather, his fur fluffed out in the snow.

Dandio had drawn his sword and was inspecting the blade. Rygal, interested, moved over toward him. "What are you doing?"

"Sword got nicked up pretty bad when I was fighting the orcs," Dandio explained without looking away from his inspection. "I'll have to sharpen it when we reach Sia."

Rygal watched as he slid it back into the scabbard. "Will you teach me to fight?" he asked hopefully.

Dandio looked up at him, that familiar half-smile crossing his face. "Now?"

Rygal nodded rapidly. "While we wait for Llyrion to get back— and maybe on the ship? Please, Dandio—it might be useful if we run into trouble when we get to Caer Sia. Besides, I've mostly felt in the way this whole trip," he added, a little ruefully.

Dandio was still smiling slightly. Then he shrugged. "Very well. Grab the extra sword on the saddle bags. Go easy with that," he added, arching an eyebrow, as Rygal whipped the blade out with so much energy he nearly dropped it. He studied the eager young boy before him. "Did Norrin teach you any fencing or anything like that?"

"No, not really," Rygal said, staring at the sword in awe.

"Well, I'll show you the basics. Plant your feet shoulder-width apart. Have your dominant foot forward a little—just like that. Now, that's a one-handed sword, so hold it as such."

Rygal, who had been gripping the sword with both hands like a club, switched to holding it with one hand instead. The weight of it surprised him. Normally, when he'd watched people sword-fight, they did it so effortlessly and calmly. He swung it clumsily toward Dandio, who stepped back quickly.

"Hold on—get used to the weight. If you're going to attack, commit to it. You don't want to stand there uncertainly, holding the sword, thinking about what you're going to do. Go fast, get in and get back." He lunged forward mid-speak and tapped Rygal's blade lightly with his own. Rygal, startled by the sudden movement, swung at him, thrown off balance by the unfamiliar sword. But he quickly regained his footing, raising the blade again.

"Good recovery," Dandio said, circling him. He held his sword loose and ready, looking quite comfortable—Rygal's wrist was starting to ache from the strain of holding the blade upright.

He took a breath and lunged unexpectedly, slashing at Dandio again. The tall Liznee parried easily, the clang of the blades sending chills down Rygal's spine.

"Parry with the flat of the blade if you can," Dandio said, spinning away. "That way you'll spare the edge from getting dinged and dented—it'll help keep it sharp during a fight."

He lunged in again—Rygal managed to spin his sword slightly, catching Dandio's sword on the flat, then whisked his sword free and cut up sharply. Dandio dodged, spinning his blade in a blur, and slashed at him. Rygal pivoted to the side quickly, and cut at the Liznee. He felt himself lose control of the blade mid-slash, and half-threw the sword into Dandio's previously injured arm. Dandio gave a sharp hiss of pain, dropping his sword and holding his arm.

Rygal felt his stomach plummet. "Dandio—I'm sorry—I lost my grip—"

He stopped as he saw Dandio's shoulders shaking, and realized the Liznee was messing with him. "I've never seen someone throw their sword," Dandio panted, holding back his laughter, "but I suppose it could be quite effective."

"It looked kind of cool, actually," Dusty commented unhelpfully from her place beside Tag.

"Hmm, maybe I'll have to implement it into the training of any new recruits for the Red Dawn," Dandio mused, a grin finally breaking through.

Rygal shook his head. "I thought I hurt you—you're not funny, either of you," he added, glaring at Dusty, who was giggling.

"We're hilarious," Dandio said coolly. He stretched his injured arm, finally dropping the joke. "Well done, Rygal. Control comes from strength, and strength comes with time. Keep working on it, all right?"

Rygal looked up at him, smiling, feeling proud of himself despite the end of the fight. "I will. Thanks."

Llyrion reappeared, holding a few papers in one hand. He paused slightly, looking at Dandio and Rygal, who were both still holding their swords and grinning. "Did I miss something?"

"Rygal's inventing new moves for the Liznee army," Dusty said.

Llyrion raised his eyebrows and nodded. "Ah. Good for Rygal. Dandio tends to use the same tactics over and over."

"Because they work," Dandio said, pretending to be offended. "Tried and true, as it were."

Llyrion shook his head and held up the papers. "Well, I've bought us passage on the *Sun's Crest*. She's a merchant galleon and she sails in half an hour. Not very big quarters, but we can take the animals, which is what we needed."

"Excellent. Thank you," Dandio said, sounding satisfied. He nodded to Rygal and Dusty. "Mount up. Let's get going."

By the time they reached the village of Badwater, the snow had been joined by a whistling wind and Rygal's fingers were freezing. He noticed another scent in the air, mingling with the briny smell of the sea that he was used to. A pungent, reeking odor that smelled like eggs.

"What's that smell?" Dusty asked, her nose wrinkled.

"Sulfuric pools," Dandio told her. "There are multiple hot springs nearby. That's why this town is called Badwater."

"Sulfur?" Rygal repeated, puzzled.

"Yes. No one knows why they're in this part of the world. If we had more time, we could go look at the pools—they're quite impressive, multi-colored rock and boiling sulfuric water. But we've got to get to Sia as quickly as possible."

Rygal was left thinking about the pools as they moved toward the port. A large crowd of people were moving to and from the ships docked there.

"Hoods up," Dandio said quietly. "The last thing we want is some spy of Kado's to see us and cause us trouble." He pulled his hood over his head, and the others copied him.

"Tickets!" A gruff voice bit into Rygal's thoughts like the freezing wind. He looked up quickly, facing a burly sailor whose large nose resembled a potato.

He scowled at the young boy before him. "Who's with you, boy?" he asked curtly.

"He's with me," Llyrion said swiftly, stepping forward. The sailor studied them carefully. His eyes lingered on Dusty longer than the others, and Rygal hoped desperately that the swirling snow would disguise the Wildkid's fur, ears, and tail. Dusty smiled at him, but she looked nervous.

"You're an odd lot, I'll give ya that," the sailor said finally, chewing his lip.

"Thank you for the keen observation," Dandio said calmly. His green eyes glittered beneath the hood. "Now will you let us pass?"

The sailor's gaze swung from Dusty to Dandio, and his eyes widened slightly. With his hood pulled up and his cloak swirling around his tall frame, Dandio looked quite an imposing figure.

The sailor finally shrugged. "On board with you. We'll tend your horses. Keep that dog below decks," he added severely to Dusty as she led Tag on board.

Llyrion led them to their cabin. It was small and rather stuffy, but it had a window that offered quite a view of the ocean. There were two cots on the wall. Rygal and Llyrion both offered to sleep on the floor, since Dandio was still recovering and Dusty was, after all, a Wildkid princess. They set up their bedrolls as Dandio unpacked the gear.

"How far is it to Caer Sia, Dandio?" Dusty asked at length.

Dandio's eyes were distant as he looked across the sea. "Many miles. But this ship will go quickly with a favorable breeze in her sails. I'm hopeful we'll reach the capital by morning."

Morning. By morning they would be entering Caer Sia—a place Rygal had never in his wildest dreams pictured visiting. Of course, he had never pictured that he could embark on a journey like this. This whole trip had been remarkable as he thought about it.

Dusty settled down in her bed, leaning against the window sill, watching the snow swirl around them. The gentle creaking of the ropes and the soft billow of the sails came distantly from above them. They were peaceful sounds, and Rygal felt himself relax.

Sometime around midnight, he heard Dandio and Llyrion talking quietly.

"Do you think he suffered?" Llyrion asked in a low whisper.

"No. No, I don't. After the pain of breaking the spell was complete, you should have seen how peaceful he looked. Calm, content. He was in control of his own thoughts again." Dandio's voice was soft.

"The orcs… they shot at him…"

"He told us they did. He was injured—there were arrows in his back and one in his side. They tried to stop him, naturally—after all, if one Haze rebels, who's to say the others won't? Kado had to snuff it out."

"He hasn't snuffed it out yet." Rygal heard Llyrion take a deep breath. The Elven warrior's voice was still calm, but there was a note of emotion there. It wasn't surprising, though. He'd been waiting all this time, holding out hope that his brother was alive, only to have those hopes ultimately dashed by Dandio's news—

"That's right," Dandio agreed quietly, his voice gentle. "Lorell wanted to make sure the spark could last, and that we didn't lose hope. He wanted us to know that we could still win. He gave up everything for that."

Llyrion cleared his throat briskly. "Yes. Yes. I'm very glad he did. But that doesn't mean I won't miss him."

"Rest, then," Dandio said gently. "Remember him as you sleep. I'll keep watch tonight."

Rygal realized he had allowed his breathing to become quiet and shallow as he strained to hear the soft voices—now he quickly let himself breathe deeply, pretending to be fast asleep. He felt bad for eavesdropping, but it was good to hear that Dandio and Llyrion both had hope. Even with Lorell's tragic death, Llyrion had been galvanized back into the determined action that Rygal had seen in his eyes many times before.

He was still ready to stop Kado.

. . . . . .

Something was wrong.

His shoulder was aching, throbbing. Something had changed, some motion or sound. In the last few days, tense with danger, his senses had become attuned to different shifts in the environment, preparing to leap up and defend himself and Dusty if need be.

There was an odd yellowish light in the room—lantern light, flickering slightly. Hushed voices carried from the corridor. Dandio and Llyrion's voices came from above him, their hurried whispers difficult to overhear.

"We can take the back road, they won't see us…"

"What about the horses?"

"Hurry, go get them, I'll wake them…"

The door opened and closed, letting in a rush of cold night air. Rygal blinked in the sudden light, slowly waking. What was going on? The pain in his shoulder, where the wound had been, made it impossible to fall asleep again—and besides, he was starting to guess that he wouldn't be falling asleep again anyway. Something was definitely going on, and it didn't seem good.

He could see the faint light of morning seeping in through the windows, barely more than a bluish white at this time. The sun hadn't risen yet, and the eastern horizon was streaked with pink and red.

"What's going on?" he asked, sitting up.

Dandio stood by the door, and turned at his voice. "Get up and pack up your things. We're almost to Caer Sia, we're just going in by a different port."

"Why?" Rygal asked, although he was starting to guess.

Dandio's worried expression confirmed his fears even before he spoke. "There's a large group of Hazes patrolling the northwestern port."

"Hazes?" Dusty echoed, sitting up, her hair wildly disheveled and her eyes showing her worry. "They… they've taken Caer Sia?"

"I don't know. No one knows. But considering I *don't* see smoke and ruin, I doubt they've fought yet. More likely they're waiting in the outlying towns for Kado's command."

Rygal wasn't sure what this meant—but he knew that it would be incredibly difficult to slip in around a throng of angry Hazes. "What are we going to do?" he asked.

Dandio's face was set in thought. "The eastern port, as far as we know, has few or no Hazes. Glentree is expecting us—with any luck he can cause enough diversion at the western port to let us slip in at the other side of the city. Then we'll ride like the blazes to get to the castle before any Hazes see us."

Llyrion reappeared. "The horses are all fine, but there's another problem. The ship's captain doesn't want us to disembark at all. He's afraid the Hazes will see and swarm the ship."

"And what did you tell him?" Dandio asked, exasperated.

Llyrion shrugged slowly. "I wanted to say a lot more, but I only said I'd talk to you."

"And I'll talk to him, then," Dandio said briskly, striding through the door and down the hall.

"Let's go, Dusty," Rygal said, pulling on his cloak and boots, and the three of them followed the Liznee out of the room.

From the look on Dandio's face—frustration, mixed with a suspicious satisfaction—Rygal was rather interested to watch.

# 16

*Caer Sia*

Kado, the commander of the Haze army, deputy of Safacon, was furious.

The messenger before him stared at his angry master and couldn't help trembling. Being the bearer of bad news was never desirable—it was a lot worse when you had to deliver that bad news to Kado.

Kado finally turned back to him, taking a long breath as he studied the man. The messenger wasn't a Haze. He was one of the many outlaws and brigands who had joined Kado's force a few weeks ago, simply because they had heard they were going to battle with Caer Sia. The Liznees, despite their popularity with the common folk, still had many enemies, and so Kado had accepted all help gladly.

He was beginning to recognize this as a mistake. The outlaws, despite being willing to fight, weren't military men. They would follow his orders, yes, but they had no sense of strategy, no respect for authority, and all around keeping an eye on them felt similar to herding cats.

"Tell me again," Kado said to him finally.

The messenger looked up at his master fearfully. Kado wasn't a big man—he wasn't even particularly tall. He was slim and severe, with sharp features and straight dark hair pulled back tightly at the nape of his neck. His eyes were dark too, dark and keen and glittering with barely contained fury. Nothing escaped those eyes. It was his appearance, coupled with his sly, slow, soft-spoken voice, that gave him the appearance of a vulture.

"Thay… didn't see us, ma lord," the outlaw said finally. His broad accent marked him as one of the easterners, Kado thought. One of the crime members from across the border, in central Daffodalion. "Didn't really look, actually. Ship just sailed on righ' by." He shrugged slightly, not sure what to make of it. "Maybe thay were jus' traders."

"Traders?" Kado repeated silkily. "Hmm, you may actually have a point there. Except for the fact that our sources distinctly said that Dandio Ki is on that ship."

The outlaw nodded rapidly. He knew better than to contradict his master. "Wi' all due respect, ma lard, it could be that we been tracking a different ship. The wrong one. Lost the right one in the night, maybe."

Kado paused, thinking. The man had a fair point, he realized. But there was something he knew for a fact. "We knew the *Sun's Crest* sailed from Badwater last night. Our spies indicated that was the ship carrying Dandio Ki back to Sia. And the ship that just passed the western harbor—the one they were supposed to dock in at—is the *Sun's Crest*."

The outlaw shrugged helplessly. Then Kado smiled suddenly. "It is of no matter. Dandio will come. And we will be ready for him."

The messenger looked at his master, unnerved by the sudden calm in the warlord's face. "But… what about Caer Sia? If tha' Liznees hear that we're here, the Red Dawn will have us like a cat on a mouse."

Kado looked at him and smiled again. The smile never reached his eyes. "I'm counting on it. Unfortunately, these mice can bite."

And he strode away. It was time to ready the Hazes.

. . . . . .

Dandio took a deep breath. Rygal could see that he was barely containing his frustration.

"I can't do it, sirs," the captain repeated stubbornly. He stood on the decks, arms folded, a lantern on the rail beside him. "Can't risk losing this ship and maybe the lives of my men if we try to dock. No, we're going east. We'll make port north of Cattrick."

"You can't be serious," Llyrion said, exasperated.

Dandio motioned for him to be quiet. "I have authority in Caer Sia. I'm a courier. The High King will pay you well if you make port and allow us to go ashore," he said, his voice level. He still wore his hood, which kept the right side of his face in shadow, hiding his easily recognizable scar. Rygal knew his presence would cause more problems for them if the sailors knew who he was. Still, they were running out of time. And the captain clearly refused to yield.

The captain, for his part, looked mildly interested as Dandio mentioned the High King and payment. "Do you now? How much? Well, never mind," he said quickly. "No one's making port and no one's going ashore with those Hazes prowling around. They'll board my ship and destroy my cargo with it."

"Captain, please. This is of the utmost importance." Dandio's voice was still level and calm, but there was a slight edge in his tone as he spoke. "The Hazes have no interest in you or your ship. Once we're on shore, we'll lead them away from you, and you can sail away safely."

The captain was shaking his head before Dandio finished. The sailors behind him looked uncomfortable. They knew their captain, while a good seafarer, was terribly stubborn and quite arrogant. He was also fiercely protective of his ship—more importantly, of the goods on board his ship. That being said, even they could tell that the strange Liznee before them was dead serious. And they wished their captain would stop being so difficult.

"I'm not stopping for you, Liznee. That's final. Now go below decks to your room and hope the Hazes don't come after us as we pass," he stated loudly.

Rygal looked up at Dandio. "What will…"

Dandio stepped forward suddenly, removing his hood, and fixing the sailors with his vivid green stare. "Hard to starboard. Adjust the sheets. Make for the port."

The captain whipped around, sputtering his indignation. "Are you trying to take control of my ship? You are truly a—"

Dandio flashed a quick smile at him. "Actually, I just did. You are a reserve charter, are you not? And you serve Caer Sia?"

The captain choked on his protests, totally at a loss for words. The lantern had lit Dandio's features, highlighting his scar. The sailors all realized exactly who was speaking to them—the captain was a little too slow on the uptake.

"'Course I am—who the blazes do you think you are?" he demanded angrily.

Dandio stepped close to him with frightening speed, towering over him. "More importantly is who you think *you* are. You are a reserve charter for the Red Dawn—do you know what that means? That means that you answer ultimately to the commander of Caer Sia during times of war. Now, I think you know that we're in times of war—just to be clear, we are moments away from a full-on battle with those Hazes. And *you* are wasting my time."

"You can't just—" the captain blustered.

Dandio smiled again, this one totally devoid of humor. "Yes, actually, I can. I am commandeering your ship and crew for approximately—" he paused, glancing toward shore, which they were rapidly approaching— "ten more minutes."

The captain opened and closed his mouth several times, realizing finally that he was in the wrong—but he wasn't going to admit it. Finally he straightened, smoothing his clothes, and snorted. "Very well. Have them do what you want, sir. I'll be below decks."

Dandio ignored him entirely, which clearly made him angrier, and he disappeared down below.

"Lovely personality," Llyrion commented dryly. The sailors, who were more agreeable than their captain, had submitted willingly to Dandio's authority and were bringing the ship in.

"Mmm," Dandio murmured, glancing out over the water. "See any Hazes yet?"

They peered towards the rapidly approaching shoreline. In the half-light, it was impossible to see anything. "Nothing yet," Llyrion said.

"I can smell them," Dusty said quietly. "They're in the woods."

Dandio looked at her. "How many?"

The young Wildkid looked unsure. "I don't know. I just know they're there."

There was an uneasy silence. Dandio looked back at the crew, who had overheard part of this exchange, and now looked worried. Dandio nodded to them.

"I wasn't lying to your captain, I promise. The Hazes are after us. Once we're on shore, we'll lead them away from you, and they'll follow us."

The first mate nodded slowly. "With all due respect, sir, won't the Hazes attack us the minute they see us off shore?"

"They don't have any weapons to shoot at you," Llyrion told them. "Besides that, they're very focused creatures. They'll see us on a ship and pay little to no attention to you as long as you stay out of their way."

The sailors looked a little reassured—only a little, though.

Dusty made Tag sit, and stroked his fur. "Stay here. Good boy," she said softly. The young wolfhound was trembling, clearly able to sense the Hazes too. She looked up at two of the nearest sailors. "Watch him for me, please?"

The men nodded. Dusty stood and bumped into Rygal; Rygal could see the unhappiness of leaving her dog in her eyes. "I can't lead him through the Hazes. He doesn't understand."

"He'll be all right," Rygal reassured her.

The three horses had been led up on deck. They seemed to sense the Hazes nearby as well as Tag, and tossed their heads anxiously.

Rygal looked at Dandio, taking a breath. "Okay, so once we're on shore… what do we do?"

Dandio was adjusting his saddle. "Ride. We ride as fast as we can into town. The Hazes will follow us. I'm counting on that. If we can get them all in one place, it'll be better than them scattered throughout the city, or possibly putting the common folk in danger."

Rygal knew he was right. Still, the idea of deliberately drawing the Hazes after them was a terrifying one. "And then what?"

"Then we get into the castle. The Red Dawn is already alerted to the danger, and should be armed and ready when we get there. And then we will fight."

"Fight the Hazes?" Dusty repeated, raising her eyebrows.

"Capture the Hazes. Stop them. If we're going to turn them back, we need them out of battle rage, and out of Kado's reach.

We'll catch as many as we can and test our theory then." Dandio tightened the girth, then checked the other two horses. "Our sources tell us that in addition to the Hazes, Kado has more help too—orcs, outlaws, brigands. Caer Sia has no shortage of enemies, unfortunately."

"We'll be ready for them," Llyrion said. He had reappeared from below with the last of their gear.

Dandio rooted through the packs, looking for any necessities, then removed those and handed the rest of the gear to the sailors. "Keep the rest of this. Take it as thanks for your cooperation."

The sailors looked grateful and nodded. Dandio nodded to the three companions. "Mount up. Get ready to go as soon as we're on shore."

The ship drew closer to the docks. The port itself consisted of four small buildings and the pier, which looked rather old. A thin strip of forest grew between the little port and the city main. Rygal could see the tips of the taller, elegant buildings that was part of the lavish beauty of the Coonsian capital.

They would have to get there, and get there fast.

His mouth was dry. There was no sign of Hazes, but he was sure they were there. His shoulder ached from their close proximity. He glanced at Dusty.

"Ready?"

Dusty smiled shakily and nodded.

Dandio and Llyrion swung into their saddles. Llyrion had an

arrow nocked to his bowstring, his keen eyes scanning the shore carefully. Everything was quite still. Yet that was somehow more chilling.

The ship drew level with the docks. The sailors let down the gangway—the planks hit the dock with a jarring thud. "Quiet," Rygal murmured to no one in particular, his nerves jangling.

"The Hazes already know we're here," Dusty reminded him softly. "Might as well be fast instead of quiet."

They rode forward, down the gangway and onto the dock. It was still quite silent. The ship pulled away, moving back out to sea. Rygal could see the relieved expressions on the sailors' faces as they left the port behind.

When he turned around, the Hazes were in front of them.

Rygal had no idea how they had moved so silently, so quickly, in those shuddering, jerking movements. Dandio's horse, nearest to them, balked and gave an uncertain whinny—Llyrion's shed to the side. Dandio patted the black mare reassuringly, his eyes on the Hazes, who were slowly stumbling toward them.

"Go!" he shouted suddenly, urging the horse forward.

The sudden noise and movement made the Hazes pause—Dandio fired a plume of red lightning at their feet, making them leap back—Llyrion spurred his horse forward in the split second pause that Dandio had offered.

Rygal and Dusty's horse, trained to follow Llyrion's motions, jolted forward in the same instant. Its hooves clattered on the wooden planks as it sped after Llyrion. They passed the first group of Hazes, who reacted too slowly. The second group lunged at them, reaching for them. The horse passed them by inches.

"Hang on!" Rygal yelled back to Dusty as they galloped after Llyrion and Dandio. He had never ridden a horse in this way, and definitely never with this cold, terrified feeling in the pit of his stomach. He looked back over his shoulder—the Hazes had regrouped, and were coming after them.

"Here they come," Dusty said softly, holding tightly to Rygal's waist.

Rygal bent over the horse's neck and they sped on. He kept his grip firm on the reins, knowing that, in the horse's terror, it might overextend itself and run itself ragged in the first few seconds of this frantic race. Then, stumbling in weariness, it would run out of stamina and the Hazes would have them. Instead he checked the horse's head, holding it back ever so slightly. This horse was fast, he knew—it could outrun the Hazes even if it wasn't at top speed.

"Watch ahead!" Dandio's voice warned, and Rygal looked up in time to see a large group of orcs emerge from a side street, all of them carrying bows.

Llyrion rose in the saddle and fired two shots in rapid succession— the first slammed into the upper arm of the nearest orc, making it shout in pain, and the second slashed through another orc's throat. The second orc fell without a sound.

They were nearly out of the forest, and Rygal could see houses and buildings that marked the city ahead of them, when a throng of Hazes appeared out of nowhere.

Dandio saw them first, as his horse reeled back with a startled whinny. Llyrion reined up sharply, uncertain for an instant—Dandio shouted for him to keep going.

In the same second, one of the orcs seized the reins of Rygal and Dusty's horse.

Rygal felt the horse stumble as the orc hauled it brutally to a stop. "No!" he shouted, swinging a wild punch at the orc—he missed badly, and the orc grinned up at him, its piggy black eyes filled with malice. Rygal didn't have a weapon—there was nothing he could do, and now the Hazes were catching up to them—

"Hold on," he ordered Dusty, swinging down out of the saddle. Hot rage was filling him, a familiar anger, a familiar determination. He had felt it fighting the soldiers in the market back in Gayrile and he felt it now. The orc's attention was on Dusty, who had straightened in the saddle. She snatched a spear from one of the other orcs, as was now brandishing it at their captors, keeping them back.

Rygal stepped in swiftly, his eyes fixed on his target, and slammed his fist into the orc's jaw. It was the type of attack that Norrin had taught him, in case he ever needed to defend himself. *A quick jab followed by a larger, heavier blow when your target is stunned from the first,* Norrin's words echoed in his mind as he struck the orc again, slamming the palm of his hand into the orc's brutish face.

The orc stumbled back, dropping the reins, snarling in pain and rage. Behind him, Rygal saw Dusty swing the spear about clumsily, not quite strong enough to keep it up. But it had the right effect—none of the orcs wanted to get close with her swinging it around.

He seized the reins and handed them to Dusty, preparing to mount again. Then the young Wildkid's eyes fixed something behind him—and she screamed.

Rygal felt cold, clammy hands lock around his throat, lifting him from the ground, and he saw the shifting, shivering forms that were the Hazes, forming an impenetrable wall around them.

"No!" he screamed, the word cut off as the Haze's hand covered his mouth. He coughed and squirmed, gasping at the pain and loss of air—there was nothing he could do, no way to escape—

Then from his left came a crash, followed by a brilliant flash of red, and he knew Dandio had joined their battle. The Haze's hold loosened, and Rygal gave a mighty squirm and broke free. The Hazes' attention seemed fixed entirely on Dandio, who had swung down from the saddle, red lightning crackling in his palms.

"Let's go!" Dusty cried. She was standing by the horse, still holding the spear. Rygal lifted a short sword one of the orcs had dropped, and together they moved toward Dandio. The Hazes swarmed around them like angry bees, their horrible echoing hisses filling the air. They were circled, completely trapped by the Hazes.

"Come close!" Dandio ordered, his voice tense. The three of

them stood, backs together, facing out into the ring. The Hazes hissed and rasped their frustration as they slowly, gradually, began pressing in. Dandio couldn't protect them from this many—the fire itself didn't hurt the Hazes, just startled them. Llyrion had gone to the castle, but it would be too late by the time he returned with help.

This was very bad.

"We'll need to distract them," Dandio panted softly. "I'll hold them off while you two run. Get ready on three—one…two… what are you doing?"

Rygal had stepped forward, away from his companions, knowing, deep inside him, what needed to be done. He faced the ring of Hazes, watching their shivering forms, their corpse-like skin, the anger deep in their hollow eyes. But there was something else there, too—something else in their faces.

Fear. Confusion. At this point in the battle, there was no doubt that Kado was screaming commands in their minds. Most likely he was demanding that they kill Rygal at this very moment.

No wonder the Hazes were agitated. No wonder they were confused. At the end of the day, they weren't alive. They were husks, as Glentree had said. Shells of who they once were. Dead.

"It's all right," Rygal said, raising his hands and dropping the sword. "We're not your enemy."

The Hazes barely reacted to his words, continuing to throng and surge around them.

"We're not your enemy," Rygal repeated, moving closer. "Your names were taken, your lives destroyed, but not by us. He's hissing right now in your heads, isn't he? Kado."

A few of them paused at the mention of the name. The crowd had stopped surging. They were frozen, watching him with hollow eyes.

"You are in Caer Sia," Rygal said, knowing the more details and place names he could tell them, the better. That was what had helped Lorell, and him. "You were tricked, trapped by Kado. This blackness, this void that you're in right now, you can escape. There's nothing any of us can do—it has to be your choice."

The Hazes hissed, a few of them pawing at their heads like an injured wolf. Rygal's words were affecting them. The words Kado and Caer Sia had had the greatest effect, Rygal saw. But at this point, he knew Kado was fighting to keep his hold on them. He remembered how bad his arm hurt when Dandio told him to remember. Remembering could hurt, he thought. But it was worth it. Grief hurt. But the memories were worth it. He thought of Norrin, who had hidden his past, the pain of it too much for him to bear. Or of Llyrion, who had lost his brother Lorell after all this time.

"Remember who you are," he said, taking a breath. "You had families, wives, children. You were farmers, soldiers, carpenters. You are not owned by Kado."

The Hazes were moving around them again, sounding angry,

still snarling and hissing. They pressed in closer, coming close to the companions. Rygal felt a stir of doubt and disappointment that chilled him to the core.

It wasn't working.

Then a voice, a cold, dripping voice that Rygal knew very well, spoke from behind the Hazes.

"Well *done*, Dandio Ki," Kado said dryly, pushing through the Hazes. "I admit I was a little worried there during the little brat's speech." He smiled. "Now I'll enjoy killing you all."

# 17

# The Choice of the Hazes

Through the circle of Hazes strode Kado, deputy of Safacon. He wasn't a big man, Rygal saw. He wore black robes that swirled around him, the high-shouldered cloak giving him the appearance of a vulture. His eyes were dark too, piercing and keen.

Dandio's face was calm, though Rygal saw his hand tighten on the hilt of his sword. "Kado. Why are you here? Come to help turn back your army of captives?"

Kado's eyebrows shot up in mock surprise. "Oh, is that what you are trying to do? Dear me, I wouldn't have guessed. Not like the little boy's revolting speech gave it all away, or anything." He smirked. "Hazes are Hazes, boy. To turn them back is impossible."

"It's more possible than you'd think," Rygal said, standing between Kado and his companions. At the very least, he guessed, he could stall long enough for Llyrion to reach the castle and bring the Liznee army out here to help.

Kado arched an eyebrow. "Oh, really? And why is that?"

Rygal shrugged, keeping his voice calm. "Because I almost was one. And I'm here."

He saw, for the first time, a flicker of doubt cross Kado's face. As

180

it happened, the Hazes seemed to grow less agitated, looking more puzzled than angry. Their thoughts, Rygal correctly guessed, correlated with their master's. To break away would require quite a bit of will power… unless Kado was distracted enough that the Hazes could remember, too.

"Were you really?" Kado said at last, the moment of doubt gone as he smiled. "So you're the feisty little fellow we nearly had near the Forest of Light. How touching. Oh yes, boy, I know *all* about you. You want to be a Guardian of Gayrile, your father fell resisting Lord Safacon, you were raised by Norrin the weak wizard…" He smiled. "Norrin is still a wanted man, you know. I'll mention to Safacon where we can find him, after I'm finished here."

"No!" Rygal shouted, his calm breaking, fury surging through him again. Without thinking, he lunged forward. A Haze stepped in and gripped the back of his clothes, then hauled him back, its hands pinning his arms back as he squirmed.

"Hold him still," Kado ordered. He drew a lean dagger from the folds of his clothes and, almost lazily, rested it on Rygal's throat. "Now, Dandio, let's talk, shall we?"

Dusty gave a cry of fear. Rygal, who wanted to resist, quickly realized that that would be a poor choice of movement, and instead was forced to be still and listen.

Kado passed the knife to the Haze holding Rygal, who moved back. They stood a few paces away from Kado, listening as its master spoke. Kado's back was to them as he talked to Dandio.

"All along, all this waiting for conquest," Kado said, looking almost bored. "We had to wait for the Guardians of Gayrile to be disbanded, had to wait for Safacon to settle in, had to wait for the Haze experiment to work, bla bla bla… and all this time, just so I could prepare and plan this conquest until there was no risk of failure."

In another moment, Rygal had an idea. He turned his head ever so slightly, avoiding the blade of the dagger the Haze now held. "Hey… hey, listen to me. You were there when I was stabbed, weren't you?" He recognized this big, burly Haze, the one that had attacked Dandio. "You were there when Lorell tried to kill me."

He felt the Haze's grip loosen, thought he heard an intake of breath. The name Lorell had struck a chord. "That's it," Rygal whispered. "Keep the knife against my throat. That's an order," he added for good measure. The Haze silently readjusted its grip.

"Lorell Tarash. You know that name, don't you?" Rygal continued, keeping his voice low, his eyes on Kado's back. The warlord was speaking to Dandio still.

"I'm not here for Caer Sia," Kado was saying in that dripping, bored tone. "Or Gayrile, for that matter. I've come for the world. My army will bring about the peace and justice that the Liznees have failed to reach. Safacon's goal is for the good of the common folk, can't you understand that?"

"Yes, I can," Dandio said. "I can tell by the way he murdered hundreds of innocent people after the Guardians of Gayrile fell."

Kado smiled, ignoring the Liznee's sarcastic tone. "They were not innocent. No one is innocent, truly. But the Hazes are the way things should be. Obedient, simple, serving. Voiceless. There can be no revolts if they are voiceless, can there?"

"You seek to change the mortal races," Dandio said. "It's not your place to do so."

Kado smiled again. "Well, then call on your mystical High Light to save you, Dandio. See what He does. He'll do nothing. Because He doesn't exist, or if He does, He clearly doesn't care." He hadn't glanced behind him, still assuming that Rygal was secure and silent in the grip of the burly Haze.

Which was exactly what Rygal was *not* doing.

"Lorell Tarash was my friend," Rygal continued silently to the Haze. "Friend" was a slight exaggeration, he knew, but it was simpler than explaining. "He didn't want to be a Haze, so he resisted Kado. He remembered he had a family—his father, his brother, his life in Elimar."

The Haze made a soft grunting sound, and Rygal glanced back at it slightly. The face was still impassive, but the shivering, shifting of its outline had stopped. Its form had solidified. Several of the Hazes around them had noticed too—they had moved a little closer, their eyes hostile. They knew nothing of what was going on, only that Rygal was doing something to their comrade.

"Remember your past," Rygal continued in a trembling whisper— the terror of the Hazes pressing in around him had sent adrenaline coursing through his body. Any moment now, one of them would get tired of him and run him through with the dagger. "You are from Caer Sia, from Elimar, from the Southern Fiefs…" he couldn't remember any of the names of the Southern Fiefs, and hesitated for a moment. "Remember your names," he said simply.

The big Haze that held him had loosened its grip on the dagger—Rygal, very carefully, eased himself out of its grip, then turned to face his captor.

The bigger Haze, along with four of its comrades near it, had a solid form. The Haze that had been holding Rygal looked different in some way—Rygal didn't realize why, then he saw the spots of color beginning to leak through on the Haze's gray and black form. Like steam slowly clearing from glass.

The Hazes fell to their knees and cried out, voices human. And loud.

Kado whipped around at the sound, saw Rygal, and his face went livid. "You—what are you doing—what have you done?"

He charged forward—Rygal saw Dandio start after him desperately, but two orcs moved forward and restrained him. Rygal stepped back, helpless before the furious warlord.

Then a dark shape rose up between Kado and Rygal, stopping the warlord in his tracks. Half in color, half gray, but still a solid form, raising a hand to stop his former master.

Kado froze, staring, dumbfounded. "What… you…"

The former Haze stood shakily. As his shape became clearer,

the color coming back to his form, Rygal saw him to be a younger man, with sandy hair, wearing the simple garb of a mill-worker. "My name… is Coran," the man gasped, his voice growing stronger. "I lived… in Elimar… I worked the mills. I was the strongest one there. You took me… you forced me to follow you… the enhanced blades turned me into one of them."

Kado gave a snarl and drew out a second knife, raising it, but a hand clutched over his, and he turned to see another half-Haze, this one a middle-aged man in fine armor. "My name is Norta," he informed the warlord. "I was a warrior, the captain of the town guard in the Southern Fiefs. You… lied to us… you promised prosperity and strength, not… blind captivity."

Kado wrenched his arm free and shoved Norta back, then rounded on Rygal. But a third Haze got shakily to his feet, a young man with a thin face and dark hair. "I was Garilian," he stammered. "My name is Everett Morris. I lived in his town," he added, nodding to Rygal. "He played games with my younger cousins."

"Did he?" Kado sneered, and looked at Rygal. "How very touching. Unfortunately, boy, you've only worsened their fate." He raised the knife with blinding speed and slashed across Everett's throat—the man stumbled and fell without a sound.

"No!" Rygal screamed, horror and grief and rage surging through him.

Kado shouted an order—five rough-looking outlaws shoved their way through the uncertain Hazes. Two of them hauled Rygal to his feet. Kado turned back to Dandio and Dusty, who had watched wordlessly, restrained by the orcs. "Turning them back to what they were fixes nothing. They have no value to me—I'll kill them all anyway. Risk your lives for them, they'll die with you." He nodded to the guards—the soft hiss of steel on leather told Rygal, with sinking finality, that it was all over.

And then a voice, a new voice, clear, with cold authority and firm determination, spoke from behind the crowd. "I think that will be enough, Kado."

Everyone turned. Striding down the street was a tall Liznee, clad in a fine suit of dark leather, his cloak blowing slightly in the chill wind. A simple band of gold rested on his brow. He looked much like Dandio, Rygal saw, and passion glittered in his green eyes. Behind him walked Llyrion and Glentree, and behind them, an entire legion of Caer Sia's troops.

Jan Ki spoke, his voice dangerously calm. "Your Hazes have turned against you. Surrender now, and spare yourself and the lives of those who still follow you much pain."

For just a moment, Rygal was sure Kado would agree to this. The outlaws and orcs he had with him wouldn't stand a chance against the warriors of Sia.

But then his face darkened, and he raised his dagger. "Fight!" he shouted, and the soldiers behind him surged forward to meet the defenders.

Rygal had thought and dreamed of battle for so long that he had created some assumptions about what it would be like. He only pictured a glorious clashing of good and evil, the sound of steel on steel, the shouts of triumph from the valiant.

What he hadn't pictured, or ever thought about, was the noise—the clanging of swords on shields, which sounded about the same as the clatter of pots and pans; the shuffling, grunting, growling sounds that came from the mass of swarming, slashing warriors. And the screams. Cries of pain and fear, the smell of blood, the dull thump of bodies hitting the cobblestones.

He stumbled back, sickened at the horror. A hand gripped his arm, and he turned to see Dusty. "Are you all right?" she asked anxiously.

"Yeah…" Rygal took a breath, steadying himself. The fight raged on beyond them. He half wanted to lift his weapon and charge in—but he knew he would probably get himself killed in the first few moments.

He looked at the Hazes. Two had followed Kado's order to fight, though they were doing so with slow, uncertain movements—movements quite unlike their usual swift and deadly attacks. The others, thirty or forty of them, stood or knelt in silence. Several of them had solid forms and were beginning to come into color.

*Where was Kado?*

The thought crossed his mind suddenly, and he straightened, realizing that in the chaos of the battle, they had lost sight of the warlord.

"Where's Kado?" he asked, looking around.

Dusty's keen eyes scanned the roadside for an instant, then she pointed. "There—he's trying to get away."

Rygal looked where she pointed. In the snowy fields lining the road, near the farmsteads outside of the city, he could see a dark figure moving quickly.

"Doesn't seem to want to stay and watch his war," Dusty commented.

Rygal shook his head. "No—come on." He lifted his dagger and started down the road, then turned into the field. The Red Dawn could handle the Hazes, that much he knew. But if Kado escaped—if he reached Safacon—

A surge of fear flowed through Rygal, suddenly giving him strength to run all the faster. If Kado escaped, Norrin would die, and life on Gayrile would get even worse. In another moment, Rygal had nothing else in his mind. He would protect his home, his life and all that he had there. It would be saved. His father's blood pumped through his veins, the blood of a Guardian of Gayrile determined to fight, as he ran, racing after the escaping warlord.

He caught up to Kado in another moment. The warlord had stopped, turned, raising the blade that had so recently killed Everett Morris. His eyes held a maddened hate that made Rygal hesitate for just an instant. He swung at the vulture-like figure, missed, and then leapt back quickly as Kado slashed at him. There was a smooth, purposeful motion in Kado's attack that sent chills down his spine, and he knew that he was facing a skilled warrior.

"Coward," Kado hissed. "You're a coward, boy. I have heard your thoughts. I know what you fear. You're afraid of loss, of Safacon. Mostly, you're afraid of disappointing your father and your ratty wizard Norrin." He smiled. "It'll be easier if you were dead—you're just prolonging their disappointment this way."

The words cut to the core. Rygal gritted his teeth and lunged at Kado again, catching Kado's blade across the flat of his own, the two daggers giving off a reverberating screech. Rygal ducked beneath another strike and lunged up, missed, and in the split second that he pulled back, he felt Kado's knife bite across his wounded shoulder.

The wound, which had been aching dully this whole time due to the closeness of the Hazes, flared to agony. His vision blurred for an instant, and he staggered, falling. Kado's face, blurry through tears, smiled.

"*You're all mine now, boy,*" came the hissing whisper, echoing in both Rygal's thoughts and reality. "*There's no one to help you now.*"

"No—" Rygal gasped, blinded by the pain. He could feel cold numbness setting in, knew the blade was enchanted—the fog was filling his mind. It would be so easy just to give in…

*Let go. Forget it all. Forget your weakness and your fear. You will be made stronger.*

Rygal took a shaking breath and raised his head, forcing his mind to clear. The wound flared with pain, but it was the best kind of pain—the pain of successful resistance. "My name… is Rygal of

Gayrile," he gasped, his voice trembling. He got to his knees. "I—am not—a Haze."

*But you can be… you will be great, powerful, stronger than anyone on Orlell…*

"My father's name was Maran," Rygal continued, talking over the hissing voice. He wasn't sure if the voice was in his head or not. His own voice grew stronger. "My father's name was Maran, and he was a Guardian of Gayrile. He… protected people… fought for people. He was killed… by Safacon. I am not a Haze."

*Fool—you're giving up. Just relax, and let the fog take you. You will become powerful.*

Rygal shook his head—the movement jarred his injured shoulder and he gave a weak cry of pain, but a new emotion was flooding through him, a fierce rage. The same that had filled him at the marketplace in Gayrile. The same that he had felt when the Hazes attacked.

He looked up, and stood slowly, his shoulder throbbing, but the numbness and fog receding from his mind. "My name… is Rygal of Gayrile," he repeated, stronger, "and I am ready to fight you, Kado."

Kado had watched with growing surprise, then admiration. The boy, despite his youth and emotions, had resisted a second time. "You're a strong one, boy," he said with a slow smile. "You'd be a fine addition to Safacon's forces." He arched an eyebrow. "What say you to that? Join Safacon—not as a Haze, but as a captain?"

Rygal forced away the last of the fog, looked up, and met Kado's cold black eyes. The fear, the feelings of worthlessness, had faded, driven out by the knowledge that he was significant, to Norrin and to his father and to the High Light and to many others. And he felt himself smile. "I'm not in the mood for joining tyrants."

Kado looked as shocked as the soldiers had. Then fury replaced it. "You little wretch," he snarled, stepping forward.

A small dark shape suddenly leaped in, holding the broken head of a spear, springing onto Kado's back. Kado lurched at the sudden weight, squirming, fighting to break the hold of the small furry hands that had clamped over his face. Dusty held tight, holding the spearhead between her teeth. "Go—" she mumbled through the steel, "run—"

Kado reeled back, into the building behind them, crushing Dusty between his body and the house. Dusty, stunned, dropped to the ground, gasping for air—Kado raised his dagger, hauling her upright by her hair. Dusty screamed in fear and anger and squirmed, but he held her tightly.

"You're dead, little beast," he snarled. And then he laughed. "Let this stand as the weak attempt to stop the great Kado—the feeble attempts of two little ones." He placed the blade against Dusty's throat.

And he was still laughing when Rygal, acting more on instinct than on any sort of skill, flung the dagger at him. The blade spun once and struck him, flat-bladed, across the back—Kado leapt up, Dusty forgotten for a moment, startled by the brief intense pain.

Dusty's hand closed on the spearhead, and she plunged it upward, into Kado's side, between the ribs. Kado gasped, stumbled back, the dagger falling from his hands.

Rygal grabbed Dusty's arm and pulled her away from the dying warlord, both of them shaking. Footsteps pounded behind them, and they turned to see Ĵan and Dandio running over. Dandio paused beside them, studying them carefully. "Are you two hurt?"

Rygal, his mouth too dry to say anything, shook his head.

Ĵan had moved to the still form of Kado. Blood seeped through the dark robes into the snow. Kado took a rasping breath, his eyes fixing on the king.

He smiled slowly, his eyes glittering. "This… isn't over for you," he panted. "Safacon will be your defeat… he will have first Gayrile, then the Mainland. He… is coming. What he has created… you can't stop it. The Jewel… will consume you… and…" he trailed off, coughed, and then his eyes glazed and his rasping breathing stopped.

There was a long, stunned silence. Then, slowly, the reality set in that they had won, and from behind, the cheering started.

# 18

## Returning

By the time everyone regrouped, the aftermath of the battle had fully begun. Rygal and Dusty, both in shock from their near brush with death, stood away from the center of the battlefield, neither of them wanting nor ready to face the carnage.

Jan oversaw the initial aftermath. In addition to being a strong king, he was a good leader too, Rygal saw, and worked alongside the soldiers to tend to the fallen and wounded.

"That's his way," Llyrion said when Rygal commented on it. "He serves the people. He doesn't just sit in a castle and let everyone else do the dirty work."

Rygal nodded thoughtfully. Dusty knelt in the snow, scratching Tag's ears. The two sailors had reluctantly returned the dog to his owner.

It was Jan and Dandio who finally led the weary companions back into the castle. Glentree joined them, his face red and his eyes still holding a hint of battle rage. "That was a brave move, my lad," he said to Rygal, slapping his back approvingly. Coming from Glentree, it nearly knocked him over. "Pursuing Kado, stopping him—it takes a rare kind of bravery."

"Thanks, Glentree," Rygal said.

Introductions were given properly inside the castle. Jan instructed the servants to tend to Rygal's wound and bring hot drinks. The tall Liznee surveyed them all with a quiet approval.

"I am grateful to you all," he said finally. "What you did was a remarkable thing, and this country is in debt to you." He looked at Rygal and Dusty and smiled. Rygal was still a little awestruck to be meeting the High King of Coonsia.

Dusty looked up at Jan curiously. "Sire… well, I have a question."

The king smiled. "Of course. And please call me Jan."

"Well—Jan," Dusty said, testing the name out and finding she liked it. "The other Hazes — a lot of them turned back, but when Kado died, there were a few still… stuck, I guess. Still…" she hesitated, searching for the right word.

"Still in their Haze forms?" Jan finished for her, and she nodded.

Dandio looked thoughtful. "Kado's death likely caused a shock for them—when that shock clears, I hope we can help them."

"It may be easier, too," Llyrion said. "Without Kado's voice to compete with, they can freely remember who they are."

"Indeed," Jan said, nodding. "Well, we'll keep the Hazes here, until we can turn them back. Allow the confusion and fury of the battle to fade from them a little, and then we can try to treat them."

"I'll send a few soldiers out to round them up later," Dandio said.

Rygal looked up at Jan, thinking. He wasn't sure how to ask the next question—it felt stranger considering he was asking the king. But he wanted to know. "Sire—Jan," he corrected himself as he saw the trace of a smile on the Liznee's face. "When Kado died, he said something about Safacon—about Gayrile."

Jan nodded, looking thoughtful. "Yes. We can allow some slight exaggeration of some of it on Kado's part — we know Safacon is not currently marching on the Mainland," he said, and Rygal relaxed a little, until Jan added, "Still, there will be blood to pay before Safacon is unseated."

"We could attack him ourselves," Dandio said, straightening, the fire coming into to his eyes. "Defeat him in a moment."

"I have no doubt we could, but diplomatically we can't, due to the specifics of the Garilian Agreement," Jan told him wearily. "Gayrile is a complicated matter, since we are forbidden to interfere with inner-island disagreements. We can offer assistance if they ask for it—since Safacon is the ruling voice at the moment, he would only politely decline."

"That doesn't seem right," Dandio muttered.

Jan threw his brother a wry smile. "Politics. Get used to it."

"That's your job," Dandio said, grinning.

Jan shook his head, and looked back at Rygal. "Safacon will be dealt with, but it might take longer for the legalities to be sorted out. Still, understand that I will do everything in my power to help, Rygal. We are all indebted to you. Both of you," he added, turning to Dusty.

Rygal lowered his head, reddening slightly at the praise but feeling pleased.

"Any other questions?" Jan asked.

Glentree stood and stretched. "If that's a no, then I've a mind to visit the dining hall. Typically there's a feast after battle, aren't there?"

Jan smiled. "For you, my friend, I am sure we could arrange one. Send word to the cooks, and we can feast tonight."

......

Rygal lay awake long into the night, his stomach still content from the delicious meal he had enjoyed hours earlier. His thoughts were another matter, full of a tangle of uncertainties, mixed with the recent horrors and images of the battle. Images of Kado's maddened rage, the knife cutting down his shoulder, Dusty nearly being killed herself in her attempt to save him…

Finally, knowing he wouldn't sleep at all like this, he got up and paced Castle Sia's halls. The moonlight streamed in through the windows, casting a blueish glow on everything, shining on a fresh coat of snow outside that had fallen yesterday. The snow covered the battlefield, leaving no sign of the bloody struggle that had been fought so recently.

He paced the hall outside his room, thinking, his mind straying back to Kado's final words. *What he has created, you won't be able to stop.* What could that mean? He thought he remembered Norrin mentioning something along those lines, something that

he didn't want to talk about. Safacon had created something…
a weapon? Most likely, he decided, and a weapon bad enough to
worry Norrin. Which, retired wizard or no, Norrin wasn't easily
fazed by simple weapons, so…

A tall dark form appeared in the shadows to his right, making
him jump. The Hazes were still so fresh in his mind, and his fear of
them intense, that he was still jumpy. A voice spoke, deep, familiar.

"Forgive me for startling you."

"Iriam!" Rygal said, moving forward to clasp the Neutral's hand
in greeting. "What—what are you doing here?"

Iriam smiled down at him. "Jan sent for me—my advice was
requested on certain matters. I am glad to hear you stopped Kado."
He paused and looked at Rygal carefully. "But what are you doing
out here, at this hour?"

"I… I can't sleep," Rygal admitted, leaning on the railing.

Iriam studied him and nodded gravely. "The images, the horror
of it, it will fade. It will never go away, but it will get easier."

Rygal nodded, taking a breath. "Yeah. I guess… I can finally
appreciate how Norrin feels."

Norrin had never wanted to talk about the battle with Safacon,
or leading the Guardians of Gayrile all those years. If his years
had been filled with half the carnage Rygal had witnessed in one
afternoon, he didn't blame him. The battle still felt fresh in his
mind, raw, sickening.

He took a breath and looked up at Iriam. "That's not the only thing on my mind, though. Kado—when he died, he said something about Safacon… about something he's created."

Iriam arched an eyebrow, interested, and Rygal continued. "He mentioned a Jewel. He mentioned a great power that will… that will consume the Mainland. He said that we won't be able to stop it."

"Well, we can assume that one of those statements is false," Iriam said softly, looking thoughtful. "In my experience, it will be the latter."

Rygal nodded slowly. It was true. The Hazes had been deemed unstoppable, and now they were not only defeated, but several of them had been turned back to their original forms. "I just… wish I could do something. Jan says we can't do much right now, which I'm not surprised—Caer Sia has to recover from Kado before we expect them to jump into another fight."

"Wise words," Iriam said approvingly. He thought a moment. "I cannot predict the future. Still, I can see there is something in you, Rygal. A fire. The fire of the Guardians of Gayrile, rekindled by this battle." He paused.

Rygal looked up at him, noticing his hesitation. "Is that good or bad?"

"Both, depending on the circumstances. In light of Safacon, I believe it to be good. Your passion will still serve a purpose, of that I am sure." Iriam smiled. "No, child—I do not believe this will be your last quest."

By the time morning came, the two ships were prepared to leave.

Rygal and Dusty had both packed their few belongings that morning. Rygal found the parting filled with a bittersweet joy—happy that he was going home, and sad that he was leaving his companions, his friends who had experienced so much with him.

Dandio escorted them to the port, accompanied by Glentree and Llyrion. Tag seemed desperate for attention, continuously bumping into people's knees and rubbing up to hands to gain pats. He seemed quite forlorn when Dusty led him on board their ship and left him in the cabin, then returned for final partings.

Rygal clasped hands with Dandio. The Liznee's eyes were filled with satisfied pride. "Well done, boy," he said, smiling. "And thank you for saving my city."

Rygal shrugged slightly, blushing. Then the familiar half-smile came back over Dandio's face as he added, "And keep working on your swordplay."

Rygal grinned and nodded, and moved to Glentree. He extended a hand—then realized there was no chance of getting away with so formal a gesture. The giant man scooped him up in a bear hug. "Well done, lad! Well done indeed!"

"T'anks," Rygal wheezed as his ribs protested. Glentree set him back down and moved to Dusty, who looked slightly wary—Glentree simply took her hand, kissed it, and bowed slightly. "Travel safe, princess," he said with a grin.

Llyrion was the last in line, and he embraced them both. "Thank you for traveling with me. You two were excellent companions."

Rygal grinned. "Take care, Llyrion. Say hi to Linwy and Alder for me."

The Elven warrior nodded and smiled.

But Rygal was startled to find that the final farewell was the one that hurt the most. It came as he and Dusty, turning towards their ships, seemed to realize, as if for the first time, that they were parting ways. After all their adventures, all this time watching each other's backs, for keeping watch over each other, from going everywhere together—it felt odd. A lump rose in Rygal's throat as he faced her, the young girl who over the last few weeks of peril had become his friend. He paused awkwardly, then extended a hand. "Well… see you around, I guess."

Dusty stepped forward, throwing her arms around his neck in a tight hug. Rygal hugged her back, swallowing the lump in his throat. "I'll miss you," she said, sounding very young. "You're… you're like family to me."

Rygal smiled, knowing he felt the same way. Like she was the little sister he'd never had. "I won't forget you," he promised, hugging her tighter.

"Me neither," Dusty whispered back. They stepped apart, both still sad, but knowing the pain would fade, just not the memories.

Rygal stepped on board the ship headed to Gayrile, and looked back once. He saw Caer Sia, bathed in morning glory, the beautiful capital he had dreamed of visiting. He saw his companions—Dandio, Glentree, Llyrion—all standing on the pier, waving after him.

He turned left and saw Dusty's ship slipping gracefully out of the harbor, and saw her waving at him, her tousled dark hair blowing in the chilly breeze.

Whatever was to come, he felt ready.

Then he turned his back on Caer Sia as they started north.

# Epilogue

*Five days later, on Gayrile…*

Norrin sat beside the fire, watching the flickering blaze. Rygal would be up in a few hours, he guessed. Fishing was best in early morning.

In the days that had passed since the boy's return, Norrin could tell that something had changed inside him. He'd seen so much—good and bad, beautiful and dark. He'd already asked a few times if they could go back to Caer Sia.

Stopping Kado hadn't quenched the lust for adventure that filled Rygal's young heart. It had only kindled the fire.

Jan and Dandio were right—the war wasn't over. Safacon may have been foiled for now, but sooner or later, the sorcerer would strike again. Most likely, Norrin decided, the best thing to do would be to alert the Direns in the North—King Makana might be willing to help them. Once war came, at any rate.

There was a rustling from Rygal's bedroom, and the boy strode out, hair wildly tousled. "Morning, Norrin," he said, eyes going from the old fisherman to the fire.

"Good morning," Norrin said. "And what does the young adventurer plan for today?"

Rygal shrugged slightly. "I don't know. I'll see." He frowned slightly. "Norrin…what are you thinking about?"

Norrin hid a smile. Rygal was very good at guessing thoughts. "Many things, all dark. About Safacon in particular."

The boy's eyes lit up. "Are we going to stop him? Now?"

"Not now," Norrin said patiently. "But soon. First, we'll need to alert the Direns in the North, and their King Makana."

"King Makana?" Rygal repeated. "But what does Safacon have? And how will we stop him?"

Norrin stood. "I didn't tell you everything that day you were swept away, Rygal. Not all about Safacon. I feared you weren't ready for it." He reached behind the curtain that separated his room from the main room and touched something he hadn't touched in many years.

Rygal watched as Norrin withdrew a staff made of blackened hazel wood. In the flickering firelight, he guessed what it was.

Norrin's weathered hands moved over the wood, and under the wizard's touch, the wood seemed to glow with life. Sparks spat from the ends, lighting the room in sudden bursts of light.

Rygal stared at the old fisherman—who suddenly looked a lot less like a fisherman—in shock. "Norrin—are you finally—"

Norrin held his staff for a moment, then let the sparks dissipate, leaving the room in soft firelight again. He looked up from across the room.

"It's time you know what Safacon's created," he said.

Rygal will return...

# Glossary/Pronunciation Guide

**Caer Sia** (care-SEE-uh)
*the capital city of Coonsia*

**Cantrian** (CAN-tree-in)
*the most common type of Essence-filled being; includes humans and elves*

**Coonsia** (COON-see-uh)
*a country in the northern Mainland of Orlell*

**Daffodalion** (daff-oh-DAHL-lee-in)
*Coonsia's neighbor; largest country on the Mainland*

**Dandio Ki** (dan-DYE-oh KEE)
*Commander of Caer Sian army; brother of the High King*

**Dusty**
*fiery young Wildkid*

**Elimar** (ELL-li-mahr)
*Elven city in Coonsia*

**Fyrocrian** (FY-ro-KREE-in)
*a type of Essence-filled individual whose power manifests as fire and light*

**Gayrile**
*war-torn island in the north*

**Glentree**
*Dandio's second-in-command*

**Iriam** (EER-ree-ahm)
*Neutral; advisor to the king*

**Jan Ki** (ZHAN KEE)
*High King of Coonsia*

**Kado** (KAY-doe)
*Safacon's deputy; arrogant alchemist*

**Kilas** (KEE-lass)
*Siren soldier*

**Linwy** (LIN-wee)
*Llyrion's wife*

**Liznee** (LIZ-nee)
*a race of silver-skinned Fyrocrians native to Coonsia*

**Llio** (LYE-oh)
*Llyrion's father*

**Llyrion** (LEER-ree-on)
*an elven lieutenant of the Red Dawn*

**Norrin** (NOR-in)
*exiled wizard; Rygal's guardian*

**Netrocrians** (net-tro-CREE-ins)
*Essence-filled being whose power manifests as ice and darkness*

**Neutral**
*race of Netrocrians who remained loyal to the Light in the Dividing War*

**Rygal** (RYE-gull)
*young warrior and leader of the Guardians of Gayrile*

**Safacon** (SAF-ah-con)
*Gayrile's cruel master*

**Sashan** (sah-SHAN)
*Lord of the Sirens*

# Acknowledgments

First of all, thank you to my family, who read the very first draft of this book back in 2015—Dad, your voices for each characters were spot-on, and remained the inspiration as the dialogues were edited later on. Mom, your love and support (and brutal but honest editing!) has been the power behind this book. Joe, Noah, and Sam, you guys are the best brothers I could wish for, and your support is priceless.

Special thanks to Matthew Warren, my college teacher who taught me not only how to write well, but to publish that writing. Thank you for bearing with my many questions (and helping me navigate the design process... yikes). Your help is so valued.

I would like to thank everyone who read this book in its early stages—Hannah, Alexis, Dylan, Destiny, Mary—and so many others! Your feedback, your edits, the difficult but needed questions that helped fix many, many plot holes—they formed the backbone of the story, and words can not describe my thanks.

Lastly, to my husband Levi. For the first conversation we had about this book, when I showed you a newly edited version, and you said, "I like it, but this might make it better." Thank you for your encouragement and love, and for putting up with a scatterbrained, writer-busy wife. I love you 3000.

All praise and glory be to God!

1 Corinthians 10:31